P9-CZU-739

xoxo,
Betty
and
Veronica

GROSSET & DUNLAP
Published by the Penguin Group
Penguin Group (USA) Inc., 375 Hudson Street,
New York, New York 10014, USA
Penguin Group (Canada), 90 Eglinton Avenue East, Suite 700,
Toronto, Ontario M4P 2Y3, Canada (a division of Pearson Penguin Canada Inc.)
Penguin Books Ltd., 80 Strand, London WC2R 0RL, England
Penguin Group Ireland, 25 St. Stephen's Green, Dublin 2,
Ireland (a division of Penguin Books Ltd.)
Penguin Group (Australia), 250 Camberwell Road, Camberwell,
Victoria 3124, Australia (a division of Pearson Australia Group Pty. Ltd.)
Penguin Books India Pvt. Ltd., 11 Community Centre,
Panchsheel Park, New Delhi—110 017, India
Penguin Group (NZ), 67 Apollo Drive, Rosedale, Auckland 0632,
New Zealand (a division of Pearson New Zealand Ltd.)
Penguin Books (South Africa) (Pty.) Ltd., 24 Sturdee Avenue,
Rosebank, Johannesburg 2196, South Africa

Penguin Books Ltd., Registered Offices: 80 Strand,
London WC2R 0RL, England

Published by Grosset & Dunlap, a division of Penguin Young Readers Group,
345 Hudson Street, New York, New York 10014. GROSSET & DUNLAP is a
trademark of Penguin Group (USA) Inc. Printed in the U.S.A.

ISBN 978-0-448-45577-8   10 9 8 7 6 5 4 3 2 1

Baker & Taylor $4.99 5/11

xoxo, Betty and Veronica

We're with the Band

by Adrianne Ambrose

Grosset & Dunlap
An Imprint of Penguin Group (USA) Inc.

Chapter 1

"Sorry, girls," the burly man said as he held up his hands, blocking their entrance. "You'll have to go around front like everybody else."

Betty Cooper and Veronica Lodge exchanged confused looks. Their band, The Archies, was supposed to start playing in twenty minutes. They'd just stepped out back so Betty could grab her tambourine and Veronica could change her shoes. Now there was a giant bouncer stopping them from getting backstage. He wanted them to walk around to the front entrance of Pop's Chocklit Shoppe with the rest of the crowd.

Veronica flicked her long, jet-black hair over one shoulder and flashed her most brilliant smile. Her dark brown eyes sparkled in the glow of the setting sun. "Oh, I guess you don't understand," she said. "We're with the band."

The bouncer didn't move an inch. "I don't care who you're dating, sweetheart," he replied. "Pop Tate said all customers have to go through the front."

"But . . . ," Betty started to protest. "We're not customers. We really *are* with the band." Her long, blond hair was pulled back in a high ponytail and her cheeks flushed pink with embarrassment. Who was this guy? And how did he not know that Betty and Veronica were part of the band?

Just then, Jughead Jones walked up carrying a bass drum. "Excuse me, ladies," he said. The bouncer stepped aside for Jughead to pass.

"Hey, wait a minute," Veronica cried. "Why did you stop us, but just let him in?"

The bouncer shrugged. "He's with the band."

"So are we!" Veronica protested.

The man gave her a condescending smirk. "Sure you are, sweetie."

Fortunately, the back door opened and Archie Andrews and Reggie Mantle came out to help Jughead unload the rest of his drum set.

"Archie," Betty called to him. "Would you please tell Mr. Musclehead here that we're in the band? He won't let us in."

"They're in the band," Archie told the bouncer. "And we're going to start playing soon, so let them in." Then he noticed the enormous bouncer towering over him and quickly added, "Please?"

The bouncer folded his beefy arms across his chest, but he stepped to the side. Veronica stuck her nose in the air and strutted past him with Betty hurrying after her.

"That guy was so rude," Betty whispered once she was sure they were out of the man's earshot. "Just because we're females, he didn't take us seriously. I mean, girls can be in a band, too."

"I know," Veronica agreed. "I'm going to get his name and make sure Daddy never hires him for any security jobs or anything."

Betty nodded. She knew Veronica's father was one of the most powerful men in Riverdale. That bouncer was toast.

XOXO

Betty was having a great time dancing across the makeshift stage, alternating hitting her tambourine with her hand and on her hip. She looked over at Archie playing guitar and singing, Reggie on bass, Jughead banging on the drums, and her best friend, Veronica, on the keyboard. The show was going great.

Even a few parents had shown up, including Veronica's father, Mr. Lodge. He didn't approve of his teenage daughter spending too much time with Archie. Or, as Mr. Lodge referred to him, "that Andrews boy." But he couldn't resist the opportunity to see his little girl in the spotlight, looking so pretty while playing the keyboard.

"That's my Veronica," he grinned, giving Pop Tate a nudge with his elbow. "Looks like all those private piano lessons really paid off."

Up onstage, Veronica wasn't happy. She couldn't help but envy the freedom that her friend had while performing. When Betty wasn't singing, all she did was dance around the stage. Veronica, on the other hand, actually had to pay attention. It wasn't so easy to play and sing at the same time, and Veronica wondered if maybe she could be a better singer if she didn't have to worry about playing the right notes all the time.

"Jingle Jangle" was the next song on the set list. It was Betty's turn to sing lead. She bounced over to Archie's microphone at the front of the stage. Usually when they sang this song, Archie would share a microphone with Reggie. But this time Archie just stood there. The band started playing the song, so Betty squeezed in next to Archie and began to sing:

Being kind of pretty
And down here in the city
Find it isn't easy to be smart

Then, when everyone in The Archies joined in to sing the refrain of "La, da, da, la, da, da," Archie leaned in close to the microphone with Betty, bringing their faces only inches apart.

Veronica felt her jealousy-o-meter skyrocket. She knew for a fact that Archie liked her more than any other girl at Riverdale High, but they weren't *officially* boyfriend and girlfriend. But still, she made a mental note to buy the band an extra microphone. Daddy had just given her a new credit card, and she couldn't wait to break it in.

Then The Archies started up their next tune, "Sugar, Sugar." Veronica quickly forgot about her jealousy and started dancing behind her keyboard. It was everybody in the band's favorite song. In fact, from the way the kids were dancing, it was probably everybody's favorite song in all of Riverdale.

Archie leaned close to his microphone, strummed his guitar, and sang:

Sugar, awe, honey, honey
You are my candy girl
And you got me wanting you

Betty danced over to Veronica. She was smiling at her so genuinely and having so much fun that Veronica immediately felt guilty for her flash of jealousy. Betty was her best friend, after all. And they were in The Archies to make music and have fun. Still, it would be nice to get a little more onstage attention. Veronica decided she was going to talk to Archie as soon as possible.

XOXO

After the show, Betty and Veronica grabbed two empty seats at the ice cream counter while they waited for Archie and Reggie to finish loading Jughead's drum kit into his car. The drummer himself was already at the counter with a hamburger and chocolate shake.

"Hey, Jughead," Betty called over to him. "Shouldn't you be helping the guys load the car? I mean, they are your drums."

"Nah," Jughead said. He slathered his burger with ketchup, mustard, and pickles. "They can handle it." He took a giant bite, then continued in a muffled voice, "Besides, I'm hungry."

Veronica laughed. "Tell me something: When aren't you hungry?"

"Never." Jughead shrugged before taking another big bite.

Their friend Kevin Keller approached the counter and pulled up a stool. "Nice show, girls. You sounded really good," he said.

"Thanks!" Betty and Veronica replied simultaneously.

Veronica looked at Kevin, taking in his good looks and calm manner. Then she continued. "You know, Kevin, with your blue eyes and that wavy, blond hair, you really could date any girl you wanted. Are you sure you don't want us to fix you up with someone? We know all the girls at Riverdale."

"Nope, still gay," he told her. He smiled wide and added, "But thanks for asking."

Archie and Reggie finally walked in and pulled up their own stools. "Hey, Pop," Archie called to the owner. "How about a couple of sodas for the band?"

"You got it!" Mr. Tate answered from the other end of the counter.

The crowd at Pop's was starting to thin out. The band moved from the counter over to an empty table. Everyone but Jughead that is. He and Kevin had just ordered five plates of hot wings and were gearing up for another of their epic eating competitions.

"Another great show," Archie said, leaning back in his chair and folding his hands behind his head. "Yep, The Archies are sounding pretty good. In fact, I can't think of anything that would make our band better."

Veronica quickly added, "Oh, I can."

Archie shot up in his seat. "Really?" he asked. "What could we possibly change?"

Veronica tossed her raven-black hair over her shoulder. "Well, for one thing, no one can see me all the way at the back of the stage."

"So?" Reggie asked. He ran a hand over his head, keeping his dark hair slicked back off his face.

"So," Veronica shot back, "I have the most stage presence of anyone in the band. And the best clothes. That brings me to . . ."

"Oh boy," Archie mumbled. He could feel Veronica warming up her list of demands.

Veronica cleared her throat and looked around the group. "We need to change the name of the band."

"What?!" Archie and Reggie both exclaimed. Jughead looked over from the counter. His lips were red and there were tears running down his cheeks. Kevin took the opportunity and jammed two wings into his mouth. Somehow he looked just as cool as ever—not a drop of hot sauce anywhere.

Betty just looked at her, wondering what her friend was going to say.

"Yep," Veronica smiled. "I mean, what kind of name is The Archies? It's like you think we're all boys or something. If you haven't noticed, Betty and I are girls. I mean, you wouldn't call one of us Archie."

"She's right, you know. We are females," Betty added. She covered her mouth to hide a giggle. She agreed with her friend, but would never have had the courage to tell Archie to change the name of his band.

Archie shook his head. He couldn't believe his ears. "Okay, Ronnie," he said, trying to restore the peace. "What do you think we should call the band?"

Veronica thought for a moment. Then she

said, "I think we should call it The Archies with Veronica."

"Excuse me?" Betty whipped her head around so fast that it caused her blond ponytail to wrap around her neck. "I sing more than you do, and I've co-written some of the songs with Archie. Sometimes I even play guitar. Why wouldn't I be mentioned in the name?"

"Okay fine," Veronica relented. "We can be The Archies with Veronica and Betty."

"How about The Archies with Betty and Veronica?" Betty countered. "I think that has a better ring to it."

Veronica gave a little pout. "That's fine by me as long as I get moved up front. I'm sick of being stuck in the back behind my keyboard."

"What do you think, Archie?" Betty blinked her big, blue eyes at him.

"Yes, Archiekins," Veronica added. "What do you want to call the band?"

Kevin leaned over from his stool at the counter and said, "Hey, I have an idea, why don't you call the band Love Triangle?" but everyone just ignored him.

"Archie?" Veronica raised her eyebrows and pierced him with a look.

"Well . . . um . . . ," Archie mumbled.

"Ladies, ladies," Reggie interrupted. "I think you're forgetting a very important thing."

"What?" both girls asked in unison.

Reggie folded his hands and said in a very matter-of-fact tone, "You're not really part of the band."

"What?!" Betty and Veronica repeated, but at a much higher volume and intensity.

"Don't get your ponytails in a twist," Reggie said, raising both his hands in defense. "Hear me out." Betty and Veronica both glared at him, but remained silent. "Our little carrot-topped friend, Archie, here put the band together. He's the lead singer, he writes most of the songs, *and* he plays guitar, so Archie gets to call the band whatever he wants."

Archie smiled at his friend. "Thanks, buddy."

"Wait, I'm not finished," Reggie continued. "I play bass, which everyone knows is the second most important instrument in any rock band. And then there's Jughead over there." Reggie gestured with his thumb toward the counter. Jughead's head hung low and his face was covered in hot sauce. Kevin downed the last wing and raised his arms victoriously. "He's the drummer and everyone knows you've got to have a drummer."

Veronica was losing patience. "What's your point, Reggie?"

"I already said it if you bothered to listen. You're not in the band. Not really."

"Reggie." Betty gave him a concerned look. "Are you running a fever? You're not making sense. How can we not be in the band?"

"Okay, blondie, let me see if I can explain it in a way you can understand," Reggie said. "A band is like a cake. And pretty girls who dance around shaking a tambourine or plunking out a few notes on a piano are the frosting, not the cake. Archie, Jughead, and I are the cake." He shrugged. "You guys are just the frosting."

"Archiekins!" Veronica barked. "Is this true? Do you really think Betty and I aren't important? Do you really think we're just *frosting*?"

"Well . . ." Archie blushed so red that his freckles were no longer visible.

Veronica stood up so quickly that her chair tipped over. "Wrong answer!" she shouted.

Archie jumped to his feet. "Veronica, wait!"

But it was too late. "No, I won't wait!" Veronica said, her eyes flashing with anger. "I can't believe you only think of us as frosting!"

"I never said that!" Archie insisted.

"Yeah, but you didn't tell Reggie he was wrong, did you?" Veronica was furious.

"No," Archie confessed. "I'm . . . sorry?"

Betty picked up her purse and got to her feet. "Archie, how could you? After all those times I helped you write songs and work on lyrics and . . . well, just everything. And you call us frosting!"

"I didn't call you frosting!" Archie persisted. "Reggie did!"

"Come on, Betty," Veronica said. "I thought The Archies was about being in a band with friends and having fun."

"It is!" Archie insisted. His flush of embarrassment had drained away and now he looked downright pale. "You're taking off? What are you girls going to do?"

Veronica grabbed Betty's hand. "The 'frosting' is leaving. We're going to form our own band. An all-girl band. And it's going to be about fun and friendship and not about being big, fat, jerk-faces!"

"That's right!" Betty agreed.

The girls swept out of Pop Tate's in a huff, slamming the back door behind them. The sound brought Jughead out of his hot wing coma. He looked around and then staggered over to the table where Archie and Reggie sat, stunned. "Hey, guys, what's going on?" he asked. "Where'd the girls go? Veronica said something about a late night barbecue at her place." He patted his still flat stomach. "I don't want to miss out on the food."

XOXO

Veronica stormed through the parking lot, dragging Betty behind her. "Can you believe those guys?" she raged. "Calling us frosting? It's just so demeaning! After all we do for the band."

"Did you really mean it?" Betty asked. "I mean, are we actually quitting The Archies and forming our own band?"

"Yes, I meant it!" Veronica said with thunderous conviction. She wasn't about to be minimized by anyone—even if it was by the boy she liked best in all of Riverdale.

"Oh." Betty looked a little deflated. "But I like being in The Archies. It's fun."

Veronica turned to her friend. "Yeah, but our new band is going to be even more fun."

"Really?"

"Definitely! I mean, what could be more fun than being in an all-girl band with your best friend?" Veronica asked.

Betty gave it some thought and then smiled. "You know what? You're right! We're going to have a great time. The frosting is the best part of the cake!"

"That's right!" Veronica agreed. "I mean, who doesn't like frosting?" Veronica unlocked her car and they both climbed in. "We're going to put together the best, most funnest, all-girl band ever!"

Chapter 2

The next day, Betty rode her bike up the long driveway of the Lodge Mansion and around to the back of the house. Veronica was by the pool waiting for her, reclining on a deck chair. She wore oversized sunglasses and a large, pink floppy hat.

"Hey, Ronnie!" Betty called, climbing off her bike. "I posted flyers on the bulletin board at the mall, the grocery store, two cafés, and Pop's Chocklit Shoppe. Where did you post?"

Veronica stretched, luxuriating in the summer sun. "Craigslist," she replied.

Betty parked her bike next to the pool house. "I put on the flyers that auditions are today and tomorrow from eleven to four. How long do you think we'll have to wait for girls to start showing up?"

Veronica squinted at two approaching figures making their way down the driveway. "Not long."

Betty turned around to see Midge Klump, a petite girl, staggering under the weight of an upright bass and Ethel Muggs, a tall string bean of a gal, trundling along with a giant case that looked suspiciously like a tuba.

"Hey, girls!" Midge called out pleasantly. "We're here to audition."

"Oh great!" Veronica plastered a big smile on her face. "Give us just a minute." Then, turning to Betty, she said in a low voice, "We need to talk."

They ducked inside the pool house for a bit of privacy. As soon as Betty closed the door, Veronica said, "Am I crazy or is Ethel hauling a tuba in that steamer trunk?"

Betty nodded thoughtfully, "It did have a distinctive tuba shape."

"What does she think we're putting together here? A marching band?" Veronica put her hands on her hips. "We should just tell her to go home."

"We can't do that!" Betty said, her eyes growing wide with anxiety. "It'll hurt her feelings! I mean, she bothered to carry that heavy case all the way over here. We should at least give her a chance."

Veronica sighed. "Oh, all right. You're such a softy. But I guess we wouldn't want to hurt anybody's feelings."

"Good." Betty smiled with relief. "And you never know, she might be good."

Veronica rolled her eyes. "Well, what about Midge?"

"What about her?" Betty blinked innocently.

"She brought a standup bass," Veronica squawked. "Does she think we're starting a rockabilly band or something? What's next? A man with a giant beard blowing on a jug?"

Betty dissolved into giggles. "Ronnie, stop," she said, trying to catch her breath. "We're having open auditions, and that means girls can audition with any instrument they want. You just have to try to keep an open mind."

"Oh, all right," Veronica relented. She knew Betty was too kind to turn any girl away without at least giving her a chance. They went back outside to begin the auditions.

Ethel did indeed play the tuba. She auditioned with an upbeat version of "Somewhere Over the Rainbow." She got all the notes right, and it didn't exactly sound bad, but even Betty had to admit that Ethel's "style" wasn't right for what they had in mind.

Midge, on the other hand, was fantastic on the standup bass. She could pluck it, she could slap it, she could build up quite the rhythm—even if she did have to stand on an overturned bucket to play the giant fiddle. Betty was all for making her a member of the band on the spot, but Veronica wasn't nearly as enthusiastic and insisted they wait. She didn't want to assign all the spots in the band before they'd finished auditions.

More girls began to show up. Tomoko Yoshida dazzled them by playing the violin. Betty was impressed, but Veronica felt it wasn't a very practical instrument for a rock band.

Alison Adams brought her theremin to the audition. "What in the world is that thing?" Veronica asked when Alison plunked down an awkward gizmo that boasted two antennae.

"It's one of the first electronic instruments," Betty explained. "You know the theme song to the original *Star Trek* TV show? It's that sound."

Betty thought the theremin might bring an interesting dimension to the band. Veronica really did try to listen with an open mind, but in the end decided the whole thing sounded too geeked-out to her.

It was late afternoon by the time Cheryl Blossom came slinking up the driveway. She wore a snug-fitting sundress that clung to her curvy figure and her deep auburn hair was flawlessly styled. "Hello, girls," she called. Betty couldn't stop her hands from immediately trying to smooth down the wrinkles in her shirt. Cheryl always had that effect on her.

"Oh, hi, Cheryl," Veronica replied, doing her best to keep the irritation out of her voice. Cheryl had the annoying habit of flirting with Archie every time she laid eyes on him. And, even more annoying, Archie had the bad habit of flirting back.

"I heard you girls are having band tryouts," Cheryl said. Veronica cringed. She couldn't stand the way Cheryl always said "you girls" as though Cheryl was so much older than everyone else. They were all seventeen.

"That's right," Betty replied. "And what instrument do you play?"

Cheryl laughed as if Betty had just cracked the funniest joke. "Oh, I don't play an instrument."

Veronica leveled Cheryl with a flat look. "Then what are you doing here?" she asked, trying to keep her voice calm.

"Why, I sing," Cheryl said as if Betty and Veronica should have already known. "Who's your lead singer?"

"I am," Betty and Veronica both said at the same time. They immediately exchanged looks, then Veronica added, "We both are."

"Oh. Two lead singers. That's very . . ." Cheryl took her time searching for the right word. "Quaint."

"So unless you have some other type of musical talent, I guess there's no place for you here," Betty said with a shrug.

"Suit yourself," Cheryl replied. "Girl bands are so last year, anyway."

Veronica gave Betty an astonished look as Cheryl walked down the driveway.

"What?" Betty asked, feeling uncomfortable under her best friend's gaze.

"That thing you just said to Cheryl. I mean, you were borderline . . . mean. I'm stunned." Veronica tried not to smile too wide. She just couldn't believe Betty had stood up to Cheryl.

"Hmph!" Betty sniffed. "It's just that Cheryl makes me so mad sometimes. I mean, she acts like she's better than everyone else just because she's been to boarding school and her parents have a little money. Your parents are as rich as rock stars, but you don't have your nose stuck up in the air."

Veronica chuckled at Betty's tone. But her friend was right. And Cheryl's was not the kind of attitude they wanted in their amazing, new girl band.

"Oh look, here come some more girls," she said, seeing a few females toting instruments up the driveway. "Let's hope at least one of them plays something normal."

XOXO

By the second day of auditions, Betty and Veronica were feeling discouraged. They had listened patiently while girls displayed their skills on the accordion, the ukulele, and the vibraphone. Kim Wong had even played "Greensleeves" on the water glasses.

"This is a nightmare," Veronica moaned.

"Well, even though it isn't exactly what we're looking for, you have to admit that Kim's talented," Betty insisted.

"Oh, I think she's talented," Veronica assured her. "Riverdale is apparently crammed full of girls with weird musical talents. If we were forming a circus we'd be all set. But is it too much to ask for a girl who can hold a pair of sticks and hit a drum?"

Betty wanted to reassure her friend that they would find the perfect bandmates. But even she had to admit that their search was proving harder than she'd thought.

That's why when Nancy Woods showed up carrying a bass guitar, their spirits brightened. "Nancy, you play the bass?" Betty called out, her voice filled with hope.

"You bet I do." Nancy smiled, her teeth dazzling white against her creamy, cocoa-brown skin. "And I'm even pretty good. I mean, if you believe my father."

"Great! Let's hear what you've got."

Nancy wasn't the best bass player on the planet, but she wasn't the worst, either. After listening to her solo for a few minutes, Betty warmed up her guitar. Veronica plugged in her keyboard and they tried jamming a little together. After one whole song, two things were crystal clear: They needed to practice, and Nancy blended well with their style.

Veronica shot Betty a look. "Are we both in agreement on this?" she asked in a low voice. Betty nodded eagerly. "Nancy, you're in!" Veronica announced. "Welcome to the band."

"Yay!" Nancy jumped up and down with excitement. "I can't wait to tell Chuck!"

"Speaking of Chuck," Veronica said slowly. Both she and Betty knew Nancy's longtime boyfriend. And they knew that Nancy and Chuck spent a lot of time attached at the lips. "We're going to have practices and shows and stuff. And I know you guys like to spend a lot of time together. Is that going to be a problem?"

Nancy shook her head. "He's trying to get a portfolio together to submit to art schools, so I don't get to see him a ton right now."

"Okay, good." Veronica smiled. "I mean, we're not going to practice *that* much, but you know how it is. No band husbands."

"Got it." Nancy winked. "So who do we have for a drummer?"

That was a very good question. Betty and Veronica still didn't have a good candidate. They'd had over a dozen girls audition and there were absolutely no drummers at all. "No one so far," Betty told her.

Veronica yawned and gave a big stretch. "I guess we have to keep up with the auditions."

Betty sighed as she plopped down onto a chair. "I'm not sure I can handle any more auditions. Maybe we should just get a drum machine or something."

"Don't do that," a voice called from the driveway. "Never fear, the cavalry is here!"

All three girls spun around to see a lanky girl walking up the driveway. She had long, curly, chestnut-brown hair and a smattering of freckles across the bridge of her nose.

"Who are you?" Veronica asked.

The girl smiled. "I'm Tina Starling."

Veronica arched an eyebrow. "And we should care about this because . . . ?"

Tina's grin grew even wider and her green eyes twinkled as she announced, "I'm your new drummer."

"You play the drums?" Veronica asked. She looked the new girl over from head to toe. Tina stood so confidently in front of them on the lawn, like she knew she was just what Betty and Veronica had been looking for.

"You bet I do!" Tina nodded, tossing her corkscrew curls wildly around her head. "And if you guys will help me get my set out of the car, I'll prove it to you."

Betty, Veronica, and Nancy hurried down the driveway to help Tina unload. They set up her drum set on the patio beside the pool.

Once she was all set up, Tina started her audition. She beat out complicated rhythms and lightning fast drum fills, trying to impress the girls. But it didn't really sound like anything more than a jumble of noise.

After a few minutes, Betty interrupted her. "Tina? I'm sure what you're playing is really good if you know a lot about drumming, but it isn't exactly for us. Why don't you just show us a simple beat and we'll see if we can build from there?"

Tina grinned. "Sure!" she said. She readjusted her position and started playing a new beat. Suddenly, all the notes made sense. Nancy joined in on the bass and they worked out a funky little rhythm. Then Betty started strumming her guitar, too, and it all seemed to come together.

"That sounds great!" Veronica clapped her hands. "Tina, you're in!"

Chapter 3

The girls all smiled at one another over the table in the Lodge Mansion kitchen. They'd spent the last two hours rehearsing songs. Now they were taking a well-deserved break and getting to know their new bandmate.

Betty and Veronica couldn't believe their good luck. Tina fit into the group as though she'd always lived in Riverdale.

"My family just moved here at the beginning of the summer," Tina explained. "I've been looking for a way to make some friends."

Betty set down her glass after taking a long sip of lemonade. "Well we're glad you saw the flyer."

"By the way, I can sing, too," Tina added. "I

don't know if you're looking for a lead singer."

"Thanks, but we've got that covered," Veronica told her. "Betty and I are both going to be the lead singers."

"Oh." A flash of disappointment crossed Tina's face, but she quickly recovered. "So what are we going to call this band?"

Veronica sat up straight. This was the moment she'd been waiting for. "I've been giving it some thought," she said slowly, drawing out the suspense. "And I have the perfect name."

"Really?" the other girls asked eagerly.

Veronica nodded. She smiled her biggest smile. "Ready?" she said. "The Veronicas."

Nancy's mouth dropped open in shock. Tina's smile melted into a look of sheer confusion.

But Betty was the most shocked of all of them. "What?!" she cried.

Veronica shrugged. "What do you mean, what? It's the perfect name."

"Ronnie, we just left The Archies because we wanted to be part of a band that included everyone," Betty said. She struggled to keep her voice calm. "Now you want our new name to be the Veronicas? That's just . . . weird."

"It is not weird," Veronica insisted. "The Veronicas is inspired. Besides"—she counted on her fingers—"I have the most stage presence, the band was my idea, and we're practicing at my family's pool house."

"The band was *our* idea," Betty fired back. "And I think we should pick a name that's cute and something we all like."

Veronica sighed. "Like what?" She couldn't believe Betty was being so difficult.

"I'm thinking maybe something to do with fashion," Betty suggested. "You know, something like Kitten Heel."

Tina grinned. "Kitten Heel is pretty good. Or the Kitten Heels."

"It's not as good as the Veronicas," Ronnie told them.

"Well, how about The Candy Hearts?" Tina suggested. "That's very *girl band*, don't you think?"

"Cute, but still not as cute as the Veronicas."

Betty felt her face starting to flush with anger. "Ronnie, you can't be serious about this."

"Uh, guys?" Nancy looked up from her laptop. She had been searching the web while everyone else chatted. "There's already a band called The Veronicas. They're in Australia. That name is definitely out."

Veronica looked disappointed, but Betty was relieved. She didn't want to have to fight over it, but there was no way she was going to go from The Archies to the Veronicas. "Why don't we come up with a list of potential names and then vote?" she suggested. "That way it's fair for everyone."

"Okay," Tina agreed. "Betty likes Kitten Heel, I said The Candy Hearts, any other ideas?"

"How about the Hemlines?" Nancy suggested.

Tina smiled. "That's pretty good, too. Anything else?"

No one said anything. Tina glanced at Veronica. "Any other ideas before we vote?" she asked again.

"No." Ronnie shook her head.

"Okay, then," Tina continued, "Raise your hand if you want Kitten Heel."

Betty raised her hand.

"How about the Hemlines?"

Nancy raised her hand.

Then, while simultaneously raising her own hand, Tina said, "Who wants The Candy Hearts?"

Veronica uncrossed her arms and raised her hand.

Tina beamed. "The Candy Hearts it is!"

XOXO

The Candy Hearts held their first official practice the following afternoon in the Lodge family's pool house. Veronica had the butler make room for the band to practice. She also had the mini fridge stocked with sodas and sparkling water, plus the cupboards were filled with low-calorie snacks. And, as the final touch to celebrate the launch of their new band, Veronica set out a bowl of pink and white conversation hearts. She'd had the little pastel-colored candies custom printed with CH on them in cursive.

Tina was the first to arrive. She carried a small speaker, which she set down beside her drum set. "Cute!" she chirped when she saw the candy hearts. She grabbed a pink one and popped it into her mouth. "I didn't notice if you guys had any equipment yesterday, so I brought my amp," she explained, pointing to the speaker.

"Oh yeah." Veronica suddenly remembered that the band would need things like microphones and speakers and maybe even a mixing board. "I'll pick up some stuff tomorrow."

"Tomorrow?" Tina's eyebrows shot up in surprise. "How? Through magic?"

"No, through plastic," Veronica said. "Daddy gave me a new credit card and I haven't tried it out yet."

"Your parents let you buy stuff with a credit card?" Tina asked.

"Sure," Veronica shrugged. "Don't yours?"

"No. Not at all." Tina shook her head. "I think my mom *maybe* has one, and she only uses that for emergencies."

"Bizarre," Veronica commented. She couldn't imagine not having her little plastic card. "Well, when the other girls get here we'll put together a list of what we need."

"Sweet!" Tina smiled, crunching another sugary heart between her teeth.

Betty and Nancy arrived together in good moods and giggling. "You guys," Nancy said as soon as they put their instruments down, "Betty's been writing a song for The Candy Hearts, and I think it's pretty good."

"Really? You write?" Tina asked.

Betty's face turned red. "I write a little," she confessed.

"Great!" Tina exclaimed. "Let's hear what you've got."

Pulling out her guitar, Betty strummed it a few times and tuned the strings. Veronica couldn't help but notice that her best friend's face was still bright red. She got the feeling that all of Betty's fussing with the instrument was just stalling. "Oh, come on, Betty. It's just us girls. Let's hear it," she encouraged.

"Okay, fine." Betty cleared her throat and

strummed the opening cord. "Right now I'm calling it 'BFF.'" And then she sang:

Finally hit the weekend
Hanging with my best friend
Listenin' to the radio
Talking fast and cruisin' slow
Doesn't matter where we go!
Cause you're my best frie . . . hend!
You're my best frie . . . hend!
You're my best friend!

"Wow," Veronica said. She was truly impressed.

"Hey, that's pretty good," Tina added. "If we pepped up the beat, that could be The Candy Heart's first song."

It was hard to imagine that Betty could get even redder, but she did. "You think so?" she asked. Her blue eyes sparkled with excitement.

"Yes!" everyone agreed.

Having a good song idea was one thing, but then getting all four girls to play it together was more difficult than Betty anticipated. Tina kept clouding the song with fancy drum fills, and Nancy repeatedly started playing on the wrong fret. Betty showed Veronica her part on the keyboard, but Ronnie wanted to try several different alterations before finally concluding that Betty was right with her original chords.

The first time they made it all the way through "BFF" as a group was a triumph.

"Okay good," Betty said. She set down her notes and readjusted her golden locks in a high ponytail.

"Let's play it again," Tina said eagerly. "I know I can do it better this time."

Veronica sagged behind the keyboard. "Let's take a break first. I'm thirsty."

"Yeah," Nancy agreed.

Suddenly a loud thud came from outside the pool house. The girls all jumped. Then they heard a muffled voice. "Quiet, Jughead." It was Archie.

"I'm hungry," Jughead grumbled.

"We'll grab a burger later," someone else said. Betty and Veronica were sure it was Reggie.

The girls all looked at one another. "Who's

that?" Tina asked. Veronica quickly held a finger to her lips, signaling to them all to be silent.

"Come on," Veronica mouthed. Gesturing for the other girls to follow her, she ducked down by the large window at the front of the pool house. The venetian blinds obscured the view.

The others moved in behind her. In a slightly raised voice, Veronica said, "Hey, Betty, that song is really great. We definitely sound better than The Archies. Let's try it again."

Quickly picking up on her friend's scheme, Betty responded, "Thanks, Veronica. Okay, let's start again from the top. And a one, a two, a one, two, three, four!"

As soon as she said the word *four*, Veronica yanked on the cord and the venetian blinds zipped open.

A surprised Archie, Reggie, and Jughead were caught crouching down on the lawn in front of the window. Archie quickly tried to stand, but lost his balance and knocked into Reggie, who stumbled and fell into Jughead.

All three of them tumbled over one another and ended up in a heap on the ground.

Veronica opened the pool house door and looked out at them. "How's it going, boys?" she asked, unable to hold back a laugh.

"Um, fine," Archie said, disentangling himself from the other boys and getting to his feet. "We were just . . . you know . . ."

"Dropping by to spy on us?" Betty suggested as the other Candy Hearts exited the pool house.

"No!" Archie protested. "I mean . . . why would we want to do that?"

"Oh, I don't know," Betty replied. She tossed her blond ponytail and eyed him with suspicion. "Maybe to find out if we're any good."

"Hey, we're not worried," Reggie scoffed. "I'm sure you *girls* sound just fine. I mean, for a *chick* band."

Tina shoved her way to the front of the girls. "What do you mean by that?"

"Oh nothing," Reggie replied. He turned to his friends and gave them a little smirk. Looking over at the other girls, Tina asked,

"Do you guys know these jerks?"

"Yeah, we know them," Veronica sighed. "And they're not really that jerky. At least," she added, "not most of the time."

Tina looked skeptical. "If you say so."

Veronica made the introductions. "Tina, this is Archie, Reggie, and Jughead. Guys, Tina is our drummer."

"It's nice to meet you," Archie piped up, extending his hand and smiling.

Veronica rolled her eyes as Tina and Archie shook hands. She should have known that Archie couldn't help but flirt a little with a new girl. And, after all, Tina was pretty cute.

"So how's practice going?" Archie asked after finally releasing Tina's hand.

"Good. Really good." Betty nodded her head several times to show she meant it.

"Great! Let's hear what you guys got," Reggie said.

"And then order a pizza," Jughead added.

"Well . . . ," Betty hedged, "I don't think so. I mean, you know, we're not quite ready to go public."

"Because you stink?" Reggie asked in as innocent a voice as he could muster.

"Reggie!" Veronica shouted. "Stop being such a jerk in front of our new friend. We just need to practice a little more and then we're going to be great. You don't always have to be so threatened all the time."

"I'm not threatened," Reggie said.

"Really?" Veronica looked him over with one eyebrow arched. "You could've fooled me."

"Come on, guys. Let's not fight," Archie said, coming to stand between them. "Okay, I admit we came over here because we heard you guys were practicing today and we wanted to hear how you sound. What are you calling your band, anyway?"

"The Candy Hearts," Betty told him.

"Cute name," Archie said with a nod of approval. "So were you being serious? You're actually good?"

"We're really good," Betty insisted.

"Way good," Nancy added.

"Once we get a gig, you guys are going to be completely impressed," Veronica boasted.

"Right," Reggie said. He winked at them.

Archie shoved Reggie a little with his elbow. "Relax, Reggie." Then, turning back to the girls, he said, "Well, I'm really looking forward to hearing you guys play. The Archies are playing Riverdale's annual Fourth of July beach party."

"Yeah, we know that," Veronica said. "I'm the one who set up that gig. Remember?"

"Sure, I remember," Archie smiled. "Seems a shame you won't be playing it." Then, he brightened with an idea. "Hey, I know. Why don't The Candy Hearts open for The Archies at the beach party? I mean, you'd only get to play two or three songs, but at least you'd get to play."

"Oh?" Betty said, her eyes growing round.

"Uh," Veronica stammered.

"Unless you think you won't be ready," Reggie taunted.

The girls hesitated. It was already the end of June. There was no way they could be ready by the Fourth of July.

Tina stepped forward. "We'll do it!" she said.

Chapter 4

The Candy Hearts made their way back into the pool house and flopped onto various lounge chairs and couches. Everyone expect Tina, that is. She was so excited, she was practically bouncing off the walls. The boys had left for the pizza parlor, but Archie's invitation of a gig hung in the air.

"You guys! You guys! You guys!" she cried. "We've only been in a band together one day and we've already got our first gig!"

"That's right. We've only been a band for *one* day," Betty replied.

Nancy lay back on her lounge chair and flung her hand up over her eyes. "What are we going to do?" she wailed.

"What do you mean?" Tina was confused. She didn't understand why her bandmates were anything but excited.

"We don't know how to play anything," Nancy said, her dark eyes full of worry. "We've barely made it through one song."

"Yeah, but it's only June twenty-eighth. We've got *tons* of time!" Tina insisted.

"We have five days," Veronica corrected her. "Five and a half, tops, if we keep practicing today."

Tina put her hands on her hips. "Don't you guys see? That's plenty of time. All we've got to do is get some equipment, write a few songs, plan our outfits for the show, and practice a whole bunch, right? Who's with me?" Her voice was filled with excitement and encouragement, but she received only a collective groan of despair from her new friends. "Come on, you guys! This is a big opportunity for us. I thought you wanted to be in a band? And here we are being offered a cool gig first thing and you're ready to surrender. We should at least try."

Betty sat up. "You know, Tina's right," she said. "I have a couple of other songs that I've sort of worked out. I'm sure if I put some effort into it, I could finish one or two of them tonight."

"I guess I could go shopping tomorrow morning," Veronica added. "I mean, if we figure out all the amps and other stuff we'll need."

Tina bounced up and down again. "Sure! I know all about band equipment. I'll help you."

Then she turned her eyes to Nancy. "Well? What does our bass player have to say about all this?"

Hauling herself to a sitting position, Nancy said, "Well, Chuck's working on some big oil painting, so he's going to be busy for a few days. I usually babysit for my neighbors on Tuesdays and Thursdays, but I can always ask Kim to cover for me."

"She can entertain the kids by playing the water glasses," Veronica whispered to Betty with a wink.

"So . . . we're doing this? We're really going to go for it?" Tina smiled hopefully, looking from one face to another. All the girls smiled back at her. "Yea!" Tina shouted, jumping up and spinning around. "Let's get back to practicing right now!"

XOXO

The five and a half days flew by. The Candy Hearts practiced for at least four hours every day. They worked around summer job schedules and family obligations. And when they weren't working together, they were working on their own: perfecting songs, memorizing chords, and planning fabulous outfits.

Still, even with all their hard work, they still sounded wobbly at best.

Betty and Veronica put a lot of effort into their harmonies, but they weren't very tight. Tina's beats continued to be inconsistent, which made it hard for the others to follow. And Nancy usually lagged behind on every song although she practiced until her fingers throbbed.

"Let's face it," Veronica said the night before the big beach party. "The Candy Hearts stink. We're going to make fools of ourselves in front of the whole town. I say we cut our losses and tell Archie we can't open for him at the show."

"What?!" Tina yelled. "We can't do that!"

Veronica gave her a perplexed look, knitting her perfectly tweezed eyebrows together. "Why not?"

"Because . . . ," Tina started, then paused. She didn't know what to say. She knew the band still needed to iron out some kinks, but she didn't want them to give up. They were so close. "Because the show must go on," she finished with a firm nod.

Veronica couldn't help but laugh. "You mean we have to make fools of ourselves in front of the entire town because of some old cliché? How does that make sense?"

"Yeah," Betty agreed. "I've always kind of wondered about that expression. I mean, why does the show have to go on? I really think that's just propaganda started by theater owners to keep the actors from walking out after tickets have been sold."

"You guys," Tina protested, "I can't believe we're actually talking about not playing the beach party. Didn't you actually form this band to . . . what was it? To prove to The Archies that you weren't just frosting or whatever it was they called you?"

"Actually," Betty said, "we formed the band because we wanted to have some fun with friends and . . . well, okay it was also to kind of prove to Archie and Reggie and Jughead that we could do it on our own, I guess."

"Then let's just do it. Please, please, please," Tina begged. "I swear it'll be fun. And I personally don't think we sound as bad as you guys do. I mean, I honestly think we sound almost good. All we need is a little confidence."

"Fine," Veronica finally said. "I'm in if you guys are in."

Tina turned to look at Betty and Nancy. If Veronica was in, she knew the other girls would come around . . . she hoped. She held her breath as she watched Betty and Nancy mull it over. Finally, after seconds that felt like days, Betty and Nancy nodded their agreement. Tina whooped with delight.

XOXO

It felt like the entire town of Riverdale had gathered on the beach for the annual Fourth of July celebration. Parents, teachers, classmates—everyone was there. Even the mayor.

"So how's it going?" Archie asked as he helped The Candy Hearts unload their equipment. "Are you girls ready for your first gig?"

"Sure," Veronica said. But she didn't sound very enthusiastic. "I mean, we're only playing a few songs so it's not that big of a deal. I think people are more interested in hearing The Archies, anyway."

"Listen, Ronnie," Archie said as he set the speaker down. "I wanted to apologize for, you know, not listening to you and stuff. I feel bad that you and Betty left the band."

"Oh?" Veronica was caught completely by surprise. "Um, thanks. It's really . . . nice of you to say that."

"Anyway," Archie continued, "I'm impressed

that you girls were able to put a band together so quickly and I'm really, you know, kind of proud of you. I know The Candy Hearts are going to blow the audience away."

"I wish I shared your enthusiasm," Veronica mumbled under her breath.

"Pardon?" Archie cocked his head and looked at her.

"I said, I hope everyone shares your enthusiasm," she replied, a bright smile plastered across her face.

Archie looked around. "Where's Betty? I want to apologize to her, too," he said. He gave Veronica's shoulder a squeeze, then headed off to find Betty.

As Archie walked away, Tina came running up. "Veronica!" she called. She stumbled under the weight of a large cardboard box. "They're here! The costumes made it!"

"Ooh! Let's see!" Veronica said excitedly.

Tina plunked the box on the ground and tore open the lid. She reached inside and yanked out a plastic bag filled with fabric.

Veronica tore away the plastic, revealing a

trim navy-blue and white sailor's jacket with the traditional flap collar and matching high-waisted navy-blue short shorts.

"These are adorable!" Tina shouted.

"What's adorable?" Nancy asked. She set down her bass and walked over to see what was causing the excitement.

Tina held the outfit up against herself and whirled around. "Look! Veronica's dad bought us these matching outfits for the show! I found this lady online who does custom work and she agreed to do a rush order."

"But I thought we agreed we were all going to wear red, white, and blue," Betty said as she walked up to the group.

"I know," Veronica said. She held one of the outfits under her chin and looked down at it. "But Tina found these sailor suits and we thought they'd be supercute."

"They are cute," Betty had to admit. "But you should have told us. I mean, we're a band. We should vote on these kinds of things."

"Sorry," Tina mumbled. "It's not Ronnie's fault. I told her we should make the outfits a surprise." She looked hopefully at Betty. She didn't want to make anyone mad, not on their big night.

"Oh," Betty said. She held up the modified sailor's suit. She had to admit they were adorable and would give the band a nice, unique style. Then maybe people wouldn't focus so much on how they sounded, she thought to herself. "You guys," she finally said. "I can't afford this. I've got to save all my money for college."

"Oh, don't worry about that." Veronica squeezed her shoulder. "They're on me. I mean, maybe they'll give us the confidence we need to actually perform as a band."

Betty felt terrible. Custom-made outfits on a rush order must have cost a fortune, and it wasn't fair that Mr. Lodge should have to foot the bill. Especially after he had paid for almost all of their equipment. But she didn't know what else to do. The show would begin in just a few minutes. "Okay," she finally relented. "If you're sure."

"I'm sure," Veronica replied.

"But in the future," Betty continued, "we need to talk about stuff like this. No more expensive surprises . . . even if they are supercute surprises." She smiled at her friend.

"I promise." Veronica held up her hand as if she were making a pledge.

"Uh, you guys," Nancy interrupted, "we're up pretty soon. We've got to get ready."

When The Candy Hearts took the stage, the crowd burst into a friendly, encouraging cheer. The girls exchanged nervous looks. Veronica awkwardly leaned in toward the microphone and said hi.

The shrill wail of feedback momentarily split the air and everyone covered their ears. When it faded to a low hum, Veronica stepped back up to the mic. "Uh . . . ," she hesitated, expecting more feedback. But this time, everything seemed to be working. "We're The Candy Hearts and this first song is called 'BFF.'"

Holding her drumsticks high over her head, Tina clicked them together four times to give the girls the beat. Then they started to play.

Finally hit the weekend
Hanging with my best friend
Listenin' to the radio
Talking fast and cruisin' slow
Doesn't matter where we go!
'Cause you're my best frie . . . hend!
You're my best . . .

They started out all right. But something was wrong. Nancy's bass sounded off, and Betty quickly realized she was on the wrong fret.

Nervous about the public performance, Tina played faster and faster, making the other girls hurry to catch up to her. When she finally realized what was happening, she abruptly slowed down. But the other girls couldn't slow down as quickly. Everyone was hopelessly lost.

When they launched into the second verse, Betty's microphone went dead and Veronica's singing quickly petered out after that. Everyone stopped playing except Tina, who played a few extra measures before she noticed that no one else was playing.

The Candy Hearts all looked at one another

in dismay. This was worse than any of them had anticipated. From the audience, there was a loud laugh that sounded suspiciously like Reggie.

Betty was so embarrassed she felt her nose starting to burn and her eyes brimming with tears. She half thought about running away, but she also felt frozen to the stage. None of the girls knew what to do.

"Come on, Candy Hearts!" someone called from the crowd. Veronica looked up, trying to place the voice. She saw Archie's red hair shining in the sun. He smiled and waved.

Kevin was sitting next to Archie. Cupping his hands around his mouth to project his voice toward the stage, he yelled, "Let's see some of that frosting!"

Veronica couldn't help it, Kevin's comment made her giggle. The whole situation was just too bizarre. They'd formed their band six days ago and now there they were flopping in front of the entire town. A person had to either laugh or cry, and Veronica chose to laugh. It was just too funny. She glanced over at Betty, then paused. Her best friend looked like she was on the verge of tears. "Betty!" she called to her.

Betty looked up to see that Veronica was smiling at her. Actually smiling! She waved Betty over to join her. "Excuse me, ladies and gentlemen," Veronica said into the microphone. Betty walked across the stage to stand next to her. "We're experiencing some technical difficulties and I'm afraid we're going to have to call a do-over." A light chuckle from the audience wafted across the lawn.

"How can you be so calm?" Betty whispered. "Aren't you embarrassed?"

"Mortified," Veronica assured her. "But hey, if I'm going to make a total idiot out of myself with anyone, I'm glad it's you."

"Gee, thanks," Betty said with a wry smile. "You really know how to cheer a girl up."

"Oh, come on. Share this microphone with me. Let's just get this thing over with."

"Okay," Betty agreed. She still felt embarrassed, but with her friends standing beside her, Betty knew she could try again.

Veronica leaned over and whispered to Nancy, "You were on the wrong fret." Nancy quickly adjusted her bass.

Then Veronica nodded at Tina. "Let's do this," Ronnie said as Tina counted off the song again.

Betty immediately felt a lot better. Making a goof out of herself in front of the entire population of Riverdale wasn't *that* big of a deal. She might as well try to enjoy herself. And just like that, she actually *was* enjoying herself. Strumming her guitar, she leaned over to share Veronica's microphone and sang:

Finally hit the weekend
Hanging with my best friend
Listenin' to the radio
Talking fast and cruisin' slow
Doesn't matter where we go!
Cause you're my best frie . . . hend!
You're my best frie . . . hend!
You're my best friend!

Suddenly everything clicked into place. Betty and Veronica's harmonies were pitch-perfect. Nancy was hitting every note. Tina held the rhythm strong and steady. The Candy Hearts actually sounded good. In fact, they sounded so good that a few teens got up and started dancing.

A few seconds later, more teens were dancing. Then, to the girls' surprise, some parents even hit the lawn, happily dancing to the beat of The Candy Hearts. None of the girls could believe their eyes. "We've got a hit!" Tina shouted.

As The Candy Hearts played two more songs, "Wonder Girl" and "Keep Dancing," the crowd kept dancing.

"This was a blast!" Betty called across the stage to Veronica as they finished their set.

The girls all set down their instruments and walked to the front of the stage. Clasping hands, The Candy Hearts took a bow. The audience applauded enthusiastically.

"And you were thinking about running away," Ronnie said with a smirk.

Betty did a double take. "How did you know that?"

Veronica laughed. "Oh, come on, Betty.

We've been best friends forever. I think I can tell when you're going to make a break for it by now."

The Fourth of July crowd was in such a good mood that they kept dancing all through The Archies' performance as well. Betty and Veronica did feel a pang of nostalgia as they watched the boys play. But they were both so thrilled about The Candy Hearts' that they didn't worry too much about it.

After the show, as they were packing up, Archie walked over to them. "You girls were great!" he said. "I have to admit, I didn't know if you could get it together in only a few days, but you really pulled it off."

"Yeah, you didn't stink," Reggie said over Archie's shoulder. "Nice job."

"Well thanks, Reggie," Betty replied. "You guys weren't horrible, either."

"Told you," Reggie smirked. "Cake can get by without frosting."

A woman in a blazer and skirt approached the group. She was wearing a pair of stiletto heels and her curly, dark brown hair was piled in a loose bun on the top of her head. She looked totally out of place at a Fourth of July barbecue. "Excuse me," she said. "Are you girls The Candy Hearts?"

"Uh, yes, we are," Betty told her.

"Hello." The woman stuck out her hand in a very businesslike manner. "I'm Wanda Marcos. I'm the Central Town Mall manager."

"Oh . . . hi!" Betty said and shook her hand awkwardly.

"I'm sure you girls are probably aware that the Central Town Mall is planning a grand reopening in six weeks," Wanda continued.

"Sure," Veronica said. "I hear Central's getting a Shoe Haven. I *love* that store. Now I won't have to order my shoes from New York."

"Well we're throwing a big party for the reopening and I'd like The Candy Hearts to perform. What do you think?" Ms. Marcos smiled wide.

Veronica wasn't too sure. "You *do* know that Central High is our school's rival?" she said slowly. "I mean, are people really going to want to hear a band from Riverdale?"

"Well I don't think that should be a problem," Ms. Marcos started to say, but she was immediately interrupted.

"We'll do it!" Tina yelled. She pushed her way to the center of the crowd.

Ms. Marcos pulled back slightly, alarmed by Tina's enthusiasm.

"Hi, I'm Tina Starling," the girl continued, grabbing Ms. Marcos's hand for a vigorous handshake. "The Candy Hearts would love to play at your mall." With her free hand, Tina reached into the pocket of her outfit and handed something to Ms. Marcos. "Here's my card. Give me a call and we'll arrange everything. But yes, we definitely want the gig."

"Card?" Betty shot Veronica a questioning look. Veronica just shrugged.

By the time they turned their attention back to Tina and Ms. Marcos, Tina was promising that The Candy Hearts would play a full set at the mall. The other girls smiled tightly as Ms. Marcos shook their hands.

After Ms. Marcos left, Veronica turned to face the band's drummer. "Thanks for speaking for all of us, Tina," she said dryly. "But did it ever occur to you that we, as a band, should decide if we want to play a show?"

"Oh, come on!" Tina brushed Veronica's comment off with a wave of her hand. "Tell me you don't want to play the grand opening at a mall. This is a *huge* opportunity for The Candy Hearts! There's no way we're not doing it!"

"Hey, girls, congratulations," Archie said. "A mall opening is a really big show."

"Thanks!" Tina said. She was so excited she couldn't stand still. She kept hopping from foot to foot.

"Don't forget about your friends. I mean, if you need anyone to open for you or anything," Archie said hopefully.

"Yeah," Reggie added. "And besides, you owe us after this gig."

"Well, well, well." Veronica shot Reggie a triumphant look. "I guess it turns out that the frosting is the best part of the cake after all." She couldn't help but smile at Reggie's sour look.

Chapter 5

A few days later, Tina burst into the pool house. Betty and Nancy were going over their set list while Veronica was attempting to open a bottle of sparkling water. "Guess what!" she cried.

Veronica spun around to see what was going on. The bottle of sparkling water exploded in her hands, spraying bubbles all over her.

"This had better be either an alien invasion or a celebrity sighting because if it's anything less, I'm going to be mad," Veronica stated while dabbing at her water-stained red silk skirt with a towel.

"It's better," Tina said, ignoring Veronica's remark. "I booked us a gig!"

"But we just had a gig two days ago," Nancy said as she popped open a soda can. "The Fourth of July picnic. Remember?"

"Of course I remember," Tina said. "It was fantastic! That's why I figured we had to strike while the iron was hot. I spoke to Mrs. Tarnell. She owns Tarnell's Gallery over on Fifth Street. Well, they're having kind of a pop art exhibition opening tomorrow night and she said The Candy Hearts could play."

"We can't play at a gallery tomorrow night," Betty said in a surprised voice.

"Why not?" Tina said with a pout. "She said she'd give us twenty bucks each."

"But we only know three songs," Betty insisted.

"Oh, that," Tina said. She waved her hand, as though that would make the problem disappear. "We can just learn a couple of covers and we'll be fine. I mean, the show isn't until five o'clock tomorrow."

"Tina! What did we say about taking gigs without everyone agreeing?" Veronica reminded her.

"Why wouldn't I say yes to this? It's a gig at a nice gallery *and* we're getting paid." Tina shook her head. "It's nothing like the gig I set up for us on Friday. That's just for tips."

"What?!" Veronica yelled.

"Yeah, at Café Luna," Tina continued, ignoring Veronica's outburst. "The regular house band is on vacation. The owner heard us at the beach party and said we have the gig. I'm just so excited. Isn't it great?"

"Sure, it's great," Betty assured her. "But you really need to ask us about this stuff first."

"But why?" Tina looked confused. "I mean, we're in a band, right? And the whole point of being in a band is to play music in front of people, right? So what's the big deal?"

"Well for one thing . . ." Veronica began losing momentum and then just sighed. "Well . . . it's really just the principle of the thing. I mean, we're all in this band together and you shouldn't go booking a bunch of gigs without telling us first."

"I'm sorry," Tina said. "But it turns out I'm really good at getting us gigs. I mean, I already landed us two, right? So, why don't we just agree that I'll function kind of like the band's manager? All you guys have to do is tell me when you're too busy to play a gig, and I'll make sure I don't schedule us a show then."

"I don't know . . ." Veronica was hesitant to put her social schedule in someone else's hands.

"Oh, come on," Tina pleaded. "Let's just try it and if it doesn't work out we'll think of something else."

Tina looked so excited that Veronica couldn't help but cave. "Oh all right," she said. "But don't book us too many gigs too close together. I'd like to do more with my summer than have band practice."

Betty and Nancy nodded their agreement.

"Hooray!" Tina cried as she twirled around. "Oh! We'd better start practicing. We're only playing at the gallery for twenty minutes, but still, we've got some songs to learn!"

XOXO

The show at the gallery went very well given the circumstances. The band had only been able to learn two more songs that they felt comfortable playing in public, but the owners of the gallery were happily surprised when quite a few teenagers turned up for the show.

"I've never had so many young people attend an opening," Mrs. Tarnell told them. "You girls are really infusing a youthful vibe to this show." She was even more surprised that all the kids started dancing when The Candy Hearts played "BFF."

"I've definitely never had dancing before," Mrs. Tarnell commented in an amused voice. "That was certainly a first."

All in all, the evening was a success.

"That was so fun! I can't believe so many kids figured out we were here and showed up to see us play," Betty marveled as they loaded their instruments into their cars.

"I know!" Nancy agreed. "It was wild. I even saw a girl wearing a pin that looked like a giant candy heart and it had the letters *BFF* on it in glitter."

"Hey! Candy Hearts!" someone called from the parking lot. The girls looked up to see a group of guys walking to their car.

"Woo-hoo!" one of the boys cheered when he realized he had caught their attention.

"What's that all about?" Betty wondered.

Tina smiled. "I think that means he's a fan."

With eyebrows raised, Nancy gave an amazed look to the rest of the band. "We have a fan?" she said in disbelief. "Who knew?" This made all the girls giggle.

"Okay, Candy Hearts," Tina said, getting back to business, "we have the café gig on Friday, so I think we should learn a few more songs. Betty, got anything original left?"

"Well," Betty said, biting her lip, "maybe. I'll have to look through some of my old stuff and see if there's anything good in there."

"Tell you what," Tina said. "Why don't I come by before practice and help you look? I mean, it might be good to get another person's opinion."

"Okay." Betty shrugged. She actually preferred working with someone on songs. It was what she missed most about playing with The Archies.

"Great!" Tina beamed. "Well I think we'd all better head home and get to bed."

"What?" Veronica was caught by surprise. "Why?"

"Because we have a long day of practicing tomorrow and then we have the gig Friday," Tina said, completely serious. "We have to stay well rested so we'll sound fresh."

"Well you can go to bed any time you want," Veronica told her, "but it's only seven thirty and I'm meeting Archie in thirty minutes."

"I'm meeting Chuck," Nancy added.

Tina turned to look at Betty. "Are you meeting anyone?"

"Um . . . yeah," Betty admitted.

"Who?!"

"A boy I met at the gallery. He asked me out for a soda," she confessed.

Tina looked alarmed. "You can't date a fan," she said in a very commanding voice.

Betty stepped back from Tina, a look of pure shock on her face. "Why not?"

Shaking her head, Tina explained, "Because a boy will come to the shows if he thinks you're single and there's a chance he might date you."

"There *is* a chance he might date me," Betty replied. "That's why we're getting a soda."

"Yeah, but what happens if you date and then you break up, and then he's hurt or angry or something?" Tina said. "Then we might actually lose a fan. We're just building our base right now. We can't afford to lose anyone just because you want to go on a date."

"There, there." Betty patted Tina on the head. "I won't lose us any fans and I won't stay out too late. I promise." Then, after a moment, she added, "Hey, why don't you come with me? We're only meeting at Pop's and he'll probably have a couple of friends with him."

Tina hesitated, but then agreed. "Well, okay. If you're sure you don't mind."

"Of course I don't mind. It'll be fun," Betty assured her. "Besides, I think you're taking this whole band thing way too seriously. You need to relax a little more."

"Sorry." Tina looked a bit sheepish. "My mom does always tell me that I get wound up about stuff too easily."

"Hey, guys," Veronica interjected. "I'm meeting Archie at Pop's."

"Me too," Nancy added. "But with Chuck, I mean."

"Cool!" Betty shouted. "Band date!"

The girls all laughed. Then they climbed in their cars and headed off to their next band gathering—at Pop's Chocklit Shoppe with their friends.

XOXO

On Friday night, Café Luna was packed even before The Candy Hearts arrived.

"What are all these kids doing here?" Veronica wondered as the band started setting up. "I mean, do we actually have fans?"

"That's so weird," Nancy agreed. "How do they keep finding out where we're playing?"

Tina was grinning from ear to ear. "Now, aren't you glad we put in the time to learn a few extra songs?"

"Sure," Betty agreed. "And thanks for helping me finish up 'Surfer Boys.' I think it's really cute now. I can't wait to play it."

"My pleasure," Tina beamed.

"Excuse me, girls," a Café Luna waitress in a green apron approached them. "There's some . . . um . . . young gentlemen over there who would like to buy you ladies drinks. May I suggest our house cappuccino? Or we have Italian sodas if you want something a little more thirst quenching."

"Oh," Betty said, her face flushing crimson. "Why do they want to buy us drinks?"

The waitress shrugged. "Well, you're in The Candy Hearts, aren't you? I guess they're fans of your music."

"Sweet!" Tina said. "I'd love an Italian soda. Cherry, please."

By the time The Candy Hearts started to play, the café was crammed full of enthusiastic teenagers. "BFF" had quickly become their breakout hit. Everyone danced when they played that song, including half the café staff.

Their first show at the beach started a tradition. Betty always ran over to share a microphone with Veronica during "BFF." They were best friends after all, and Betty had written the song about their friendship. Being onstage with a bunch of girls and playing music for an appreciative crowd just felt so good. Betty couldn't get over how much fun she was having.

After The Candy Hearts finished their set (all of eight tunes even with doubling up on the choruses), the crowd started chanting, "BFF! BFF!" so they decided to play that song again.

"Our first encore!" Tina shouted as the crowd whooped enthusiastically to the opening notes.

By the time the evening was over and they had divided the tips evenly between band members, each girl was walking home with fifty-two dollars and forty-eight cents. "This pays better than babysitting!" Nancy exclaimed, pocketing her cut.

"Well good, because the owner just said we could come back on Wednesday," Tina told them. "And did I tell you guys that I booked us for the Midvale Street Festival next Saturday?"

"Uh, no, you didn't," Veronica told her in a

slightly irritated tone. "And we can't go. Betty and I already have plans to go out with Archie and Reggie."

"We're going to the beach," Betty explained. "Archie's teaching us how to surf."

"Sorry, you guys, but you're going to have to cancel. I mean, we agreed that you would tell me if you were busy, right? And I already booked the show," Tina insisted. "I mean, you can see those guys anytime, right? They could even come to the festival and watch us play if they want to see you."

"But I hate canceling on people," Betty said in a quiet voice. And, if she was completely honest, she kind of missed hanging out with the boys. Now that they were in separate bands, she and Veronica barely saw Archie and Reggie and Jughead.

"Sure, so do I," Tina agreed. "That's why we really can't cancel on the Midvale Street Festival, right? I mean, it would look bad and, you know, kind of tarnish the band's reputation."

Veronica rolled her eyes and sighed. "Fine,

we'll cancel our dates. But take it easy with booking so many gigs. Okay, Tina? I mean, we're in this band for fun. And it is superfun. But I don't want to eat, drink, and breathe the band. Got it?"

"Sure," Tina said reassuringly. "I understand. I mean, I want to have a life outside the band, too, you know."

"Well, I'm sure it's hard being new in town," Betty said, giving her shoulder a squeeze, "But don't worry, Riverdale is full of nice people."

"You know," Veronica added, "I was going to invite Betty to go shopping tomorrow morning before practice. Why don't you join us?"

"Oh," Betty said, looking a little embarrassed. "Sorry, Ronnie. Tina and I had already planned to work on some new songs."

This piece of information stung Veronica a little and she wasn't sure why. Betty was obviously allowed to do what she wanted, but Veronica felt that it was a little strange that she'd made plans with Tina and didn't tell her. "Well . . . no problem," Veronica mumbled. "We can go shopping some other time."

Betty could immediately tell that Veronica was feeling a little left out. "I know! Why don't we all go shopping? You know, as a break from the band? What do you think, Tina?"

"Sure! Sounds fabulous."

"How about you, Nancy?" Betty asked.

"Sorry," she shook her head, causing her tightly coiled black curls to bounce. "Chuck finally finished his oil painting, and I want to spend some time with him before he launches himself at some giant mural or something."

XOXO

The mall was unusually crowded with teenagers for early on a Saturday morning, and everyone seemed to recognize the band. The girls had trouble moving through the crowds. Everyone wanted to stop and talk to them.

"Doesn't anyone sleep in anymore?" Betty asked.

"Hey, Candy Hearts!" a group of guys called to them before scurrying into the sporting goods store.

"Ah, our public has found us," Veronica said, preening. Then she broke down into giggles.

Betty squinted after the boys. "I don't think those guys even go to Riverdale," she said. "I wonder how they know about The Candy Hearts."

The three of them headed over to Kim's Boutique to browse for accessories. "Hello, young ladies," the well-groomed woman behind the counter said as they entered the shop. "Are you looking for anything special? Oh wait. I recognize you. Didn't you girls play at the Fourth of July picnic?"

"Yep, that was us," Tina told her, a proud smile on her face.

"You girls were just charming," the woman said. "Listen, I just got these scarves in." She pointed toward a basket piled high with scarves in vivid jewel tones. "Why don't you girls each take one? If people see you wearing them around the mall, it'll help promote my shop."

"That's awfully nice of you," Betty told her, "but I really don't think we could take them without paying."

"Of course we could," Tina interrupted her. She plucked an emerald green scarf out of the basket and wrapped it around her neck. "These are lovely. We'll definitely wear them around the mall to help promote your shop."

"Ronnie?" Betty turned to confer with her best friend.

"Well," Veronica said. She ran her fingers over the fabric of a deep-violet scarf. "These *are* really pretty."

Ten minutes later, The Candy Hearts left the boutique each wearing a new scarf. "I can't believe she even gave us one for Nancy," Betty said, admiring the bright blue scarf the woman had insisted she tuck in her purse for their bass player. "That was really nice of her."

Tina danced about with excitement. "Isn't shopping as a celebrity fun? I feel like we're totally famous already."

"Well I wouldn't go quite that far," Veronica told her. "But I guess The Candy Hearts are building up some local recognition."

"Anyway, come on, you guys," Tina said. "There are some outfits I want to show you that I think would be perfect for the Midvale Street Festival."

Chapter 6

"BFF! BFF!" the crowd chanted. The Candy Hearts had just finished their set at the Midvale Street Festival, but the crowd didn't want them to stop playing.

From where they stood offstage, Betty peeked out at the audience. "That sure is a lot of people. Did any of you think *that* many people lived in Midvale? I thought it was about the same size as Riverdale."

The crowd kept carrying on. "BFF! BFF!"

"I don't think they're going to stop," Nancy said. She straightened her skirt. Veronica's dad had been nice enough to buy them all coordinated luau outfits in beautiful tropical patterns. "What do you think we should do?"

Tina stared out at the crowd. "I think we'd better get back out there. I mean, we wouldn't want to disappoint our fans or anything, right?"

"Maybe we'd better check with the event coordinator first," Betty cautioned. "I mean, we don't want to delay the other acts."

Just as the words left her mouth, a haggard-looking man in a wrinkled suit rushed up to them. "Candy Hearts!" he barked.

"Yes?" The girls collectively turned to look at him.

"Would you girls get back out there and play this 'BFF' whatever-it-is already so the rest of the show can move forward?" he barked.

"You want us to do an encore?" Tina was delighted.

"Yes! An encore. Whatever. Just get back out there!" the man said, ushering them back onstage.

"Come on, girls!" Tina cried as she led them back to their spots.

Betty jogged over to share a microphone with Veronica as they launched into the opening chords of "BFF." The crowd went wild, cheering and clapping. It was exhilarating. The girls smiled at one another, sharing a look of sheer enjoyment as they both leaned into the microphone and sang:

'Cause you're my best frie . . . hend!

You're my best frie . . . hend!

You're my best friend!

Being in a band had turned out to be a lot more work than Betty and Veronica had anticipated. Or, at least, being in a band with Tina had turned out to be a lot more work than they'd anticipated because she kept booking them gigs every other second. And she would have booked even more if the other members of The Candy Hearts hadn't protested.

Still, they were developing quite the fan following, and not just kids from Riverdale. Plus they were earning good money, they were given free muffins and sandwiches and trinkets all over town, and, Betty had to admit, it was fun being recognized as part of the group. Even if it did make her feel really embarrassed every time someone asked, "Hey, are you in The Candy Hearts?"

"Hey, Betty Crocker." Veronica walked over to chat while they were packing up their gear after their encore. "Do you want to do something tomorrow? Just hang out or whatever? I feel like we haven't really had any best friend time ever since we started The Candy Hearts."

"Oh, I know," Betty agreed. She really was starting to miss having the free time just to lounge by the pool with Veronica and look at magazines or whatever.

"So that's a yes?" Veronica looked pleased.

"Uh, no. I'm sorry, Ronnie. I told Tina we'd work on some new songs."

Veronica frowned, knitting her dark eyebrows together. "How many new songs do we need?"

"I know," Betty said. She knew her friend was upset, but she hated to back out on plans. She just wanted to ease the situation for the moment. "But Tina says she has this really great idea for a song and she wants my opinion on it."

"You know, Betty, I feel like every time I ask

you to do something lately you've already got plans with Tina." Veronica crossed her arms over her chest.

"I'm sorry, Ronnie," Betty said with a sigh. "Tell you what. I'll come over after I finish up with Tina and we'll hang out."

"Okay," Veronica relented. "Sorry if I'm being a bit of a crab. I think I'm just tired from playing so many shows."

"I know," Betty had to agree. "How do famous musicians do it? I mean, two gigs a week and I'm pooped. Three gigs and I'm exhausted!"

XOXO

It was a perfect July day. Betty hummed the new song she'd worked out with Tina as she pedaled her bike toward Veronica's house. It had been difficult not to invite Tina to join them, but now Betty was glad that she didn't.

With Tina, every conversation was always about the band. Gigs, practice, outfits, publicity—all day, all the time. But now Betty just wanted to relax, work on her suntan, chat with Veronica, and not think about The Candy Hearts for a few hours.

"Hey, Ronnie!" she called from the driveway as she cruised to a stop.

Veronica waved to her from where she was lounging poolside. "How's the new song? Any good?"

"Not bad," Betty had to admit. Tina had talent.

"Did you bring your suit?" Veronica asked as she got up to greet her friend. "I was thinking we could just relax and soak up some sun."

"Sounds perfect!" Betty pulled her bag out of the bike's basket. "I come bikini-ready."

"Great! Get changed and I'll ring for some ice tea and maybe a few sandwiches," Veronica said.

Even though they'd been best friends since they were four, Betty never quite got used to the fact that Mr. Lodge kept a butler that would bring Veronica whatever she wanted, whenever she wanted. At the Cooper household, if Betty wanted a sandwich, she had to make it herself.

A few minutes later they were happily sitting poolside with a stack of magazines, plenty of sunblock, and refreshments on the way. "Ah, this is the life," Veronica sighed, slouching under a large hat and oversized sunglasses.

"It's good to take a break," Betty agreed as she sat on the pool's edge, dangling her feet in the water. Dark sunglasses were perched on her nose, and her long, blond hair was tucked up under a straw hat. "It's just nice to take an afternoon and not worry about the band."

"BFF!" someone shouted.

Veronica sat up and looked around. "Did you hear that?"

Some bushes rustled and suddenly a young guy appeared holding a camera. "Hey, Candy Hearts, why don't you take off those hats and sunglasses so I can get a photo," he said, raising the camera to his face.

Startled, Veronica hopped to her feet. "What are you doing here? Get out of my yard! You're trespassing!"

"Oh, come on," the boy pleaded. "One photo!"

"No!" Betty shouted. "Get out of here right now!" She splashed some water at him.

"Is there a problem, miss?" the butler said as he hurried out of the house carrying a broom. He must have heard the shouting.

"Yes, there's a problem!" Veronica informed him. "This creep snuck into the yard and is trying to take our photo."

"Sir!" the butler called out. "I'm afraid I must ask you to leave."

"Hey, come on! I'm a fan!" the boy insisted, even though he did start backing toward the hedge.

"That doesn't give you the right to trespass on private property," the butler informed him. He gestured toward the driveway with the broom. "If you want to see The Candy Hearts, then I suggest you attend a show."

"You're totally not being cool!" the kid informed them before sprinting off across the neighbor's backyard.

"Shall I call the police, miss?" the butler asked, lowering the broom.

"No," Veronica answered quickly. "I don't think that will be necessary, but thank you for saving us."

"My pleasure," he replied. Then he turned and headed stiffly back into the house.

"That was so weird," Betty said, toweling off her legs. "I mean, what gives him the right to spy on us just because he likes our music? What a jerk!"

"How did he even figure out where I live?" Veronica fumed. Then, after looking around the yard for a moment, she added, "I'm feeling kind of weird about this whole thing. Like somebody's spying on us right now. Let's go inside and just watch a movie or something."

"Good idea," Betty said, grabbing her stuff. "I can't even imagine what it must be like to be really famous. People hassling you all the time. I don't think I'd like that at all."

"I don't know about that," Veronica said. "I mean, it would be supercool to have your photo in a bunch of magazines."

Betty laughed. She thought that would be pretty cool, but she also didn't mind being able to plop on the couch for an afternoon of movies with her best friend. She didn't think celebrities had a lot of time to do that.

They'd only been watching movies for about twenty minutes when Tina called. "Hey, what are you up to?" she chirped over the receiver.

Veronica wasted no time before telling her about the boy in the bushes.

"That's so neat!" Tina crowed when the story was finished.

"Neat?" Veronica asked, confused. "You think that was *neat*?"

"Sure! Maybe he was a reporter."

"Why would he be a reporter?" Veronica wondered. "I think he was just a stalker."

"Oh, that's too bad." Tina sounded mildly deflated. "Well, anyway, I was wondering what you and Betty are doing for dinner. Want to grab a burger or something?"

"Sorry, Teeny, we're going out with Archie and Reggie."

"And Jughead," Betty reminded her.

"And Jughead," Veronica said into the phone. "Hey, if you want to join us, you can be Jughead's date."

"Jughead?" Tina repeated somewhat skeptically.

"Sure," Veronica laughed. "Just keep your hands and feet away from his mouth while he's eating and everything should be fine."

"Why would I put my hands near his mouth?" Tina wanted to know.

"You wouldn't on purpose," Veronica told her, "but just trust me."

"Okay," Tina finally agreed. "Hey, why don't we see if Nancy and Chuck want to join us?"

Veronica told Betty about Tina's suggestion. The girls looked at each other, then cried, "Band date!" before dissolving into giggles.

XOXO

Milano's Italian Restaurant was packed by the time The Candy Hearts and The Archies plus Chuck arrived. "You come on zee busy night," the maître d' told them as he showed them to their table. "I hear zhere is, how you say, zee famous music group is coming to eat."

"Really? Someone famous?" Betty's eyes grew round. "I wonder who it is." They all took a seat and their waiter handed around the menus.

Plink! The sharp noise made Betty jerk away

from the plate that was sitting in front of her. "What was that?" she said, looking around her table setting for whatever had caused the noise. *Plink!* It happened again.

"What the . . ." Betty's eyes fell on a small, pastel object. She picked it up. It was a conversation heart with the words "luv you" written on it. "Somebody just threw this at me," she said, holding up the candy and scanning the dining room.

"What is it?" Veronica squinted across the table, sensing that Betty was upset. "Is that candy?"

"Yeah," Reggie replied. "Someone just threw this at her." He glared around the room. "And this is supposed to be a nice restaurant."

"Ouch." Betty put her hand to the side of her head and found another heart tangled in her hair.

"Whoever's doing that better cut it out!" Reggie growled at the other diners.

Jughead leaned across the table. "Don't worry, Betty, I'll get rid of that for you." He plucked the heart from her hands and popped it in his mouth. "There you go. No more problems. Although," he added, crunching the heart between his teeth, "I wish your fans would throw something a little more substantial. Like hamburgers."

Betty excused herself and stood up.

Tina followed Betty to the lady's room. "Are you okay?" she asked. She could tell something was bothering her friend.

"I'm fine," Betty assured her as she took a seat on a small couch in a little powder room. "It's just, people are acting so weird about the band. I mean, so we play a little music. That's no reason to stalk us and ruin our dinner. Don't you think it's strange?"

"Well I don't think chucking candy at someone because you like their band is normal," Tina said, taking a seat next to her. "But you should really think of it as a compliment, right?" She nudged Betty with her shoulder. "Come on. We're living the dream. We're in a band. We've got a rapidly growing fan base that are, you know, willing to give us candy. If you ask me, we're two steps away from a record contract. I'm personally thrilled that we have fans. You've just got to learn to enjoy it."

"You're right," Betty replied. "I am being kind of a baby. But I just wish I knew how the fans keep finding us. I mean, it's one thing to know where we're playing and turn up to see the show, but how did they find us at dinner?"

"Hey," Tina said with a wink, "don't underestimate the drawing power of The Candy Hearts."

"Is everything okay?" Veronica asked when the two of them got back to the table.

"Fine," Betty told her. "I just don't have much of a sweet tooth."

"Any of you girls going to order the steak?" Jughead asked, changing the subject. "Because if you do and then you find you can't finish it, I'd be happy to help you out with the rest."

Tina blinked at Jughead and laughed. "And people accuse me of being single-minded."

Chapter 7

"I can't wait for the Central Town Mall to reopen," Tina said with a skip in her step.

"Oh I know." Veronica couldn't agree more. "The Shoe Haven, Unlimited—it's going to be great! I mean, this mall is nice," she said, gesturing toward the food court at Riverdale Mall. They had just purchased soft pretzels and were now looking for a table, "but Central Town Mall is really bringing in a lot of great stores."

Tina gave her a funny look. "I didn't mean because of the shopping, silly. I meant because The Candy Hearts are going to be the featured band for the grand reopening. That's a pretty big deal, right?"

Veronica shrugged. "I guess."

"Come on! Think about it. You know there are going to be reporters there. I mean, at least local ones, right? I bet we get our picture in the paper."

"Really?"

"Yes! I think we can leverage this mall gig into getting bigger and better shows. Like shows all over the state," Tina insisted. "I mean, it really is kind of a big deal. We're going to have to sound fabulous. And look fabulous, too, right?"

Veronica thought things over while she chewed a bite of her pretzel. "I guess you're right," she agreed. "I mean, reporters don't necessarily come out for Fourth of July picnics or street festivals, but they definitely come out for grand openings."

"That's because they want the mall to advertise in their papers," Tina told her.

"So," Veronica went on, "I guess there is a pretty good chance The Candy Hearts will end up in the paper."

"Oh I think there's a very good chance."

"We probably should go back to Marlene's Boutique and get those minidresses and leggings we were looking at earlier," Veronica suggested.

"I thought you said they were too expensive and Betty would freak out."

"Well . . ." Veronica paused to give it some more thought, and then nodded her head, making the decision to break out her credit card. "What Betty doesn't know won't hurt her. We'll just clip off the price tags and put them in a bag from Forever Seventeen. Then we'll tell her we had a coupon or something."

Tina laughed. "I can't believe you have to go through all that just to placate Betty. She's kind of a goody-two-shoes, isn't she?"

"No, not really," Veronica said. "I mean, some people might think she's a bit of a goody-two-shoes, but she's really just conscientious. And that's part of what I like about her. She's just being considerate."

"And you don't mind keeping this a secret from Betty?"

"I don't normally keep secrets from Betty," Veronica said. "But we don't want to look like a bunch of girls who just grabbed clothes out of some bargain basement, either. So I think it's fine if we fudge the truth a little. I mean, just this one time."

"Yay!" Tina clapped her hands. "That's great! Those outfits are so supercute. We're going to look fabulous!" Then she looked at her watch. "We should hurry up, though."

"Why's that?" Veronica asked.

"I've got to meet Betty in a little bit. We're going to work on some new songs."

"Oh, I see," Veronica said very slowly. She had called Betty earlier to see if she wanted to go to the mall, but her friend had said she was busy all day. She hadn't mentioned anything about getting together with Tina.

"Do you want to join us? I mean, I don't know if you're into that kind of thing, but writing songs with Betty is really fun."

"I'm sure it is, but no thanks."

"Well we'll see you at band practice tonight, anyway."

"Tonight?" Veronica raised her eyebrows in surprise. "No, you won't. I've got dinner with my parents at the club tonight. Remember? Practice is tomorrow."

"It is?" Tina squinted at her, trying to remember what they'd agreed on.

"Hey!" a young guy walked up to them. "I know you guys. You're in The Candy Hearts, right?"

"That's right!" Tina said with a sparkle in her voice. "Are you a fan of our band?"

"You bet I am!" the kid responded. "Hey, hold on a minute," he said, fishing his cell phone out of his baggy jeans. "I want to get a photo."

"Maybe some other time," Veronica said, quickly stepping around him. "We're in a bit of a hurry."

"Oh, come on, Veronica. We're not in *that* big of a hurry," Tina told her.

Veronica was not in the mood to deal with posing for a picture while some boy drooled over her. In fact, she wasn't in a very good mood at all.

"Sorry," she said. "We'll catch you some other time. Remind me and we'll pose for a picture at one of our shows. With the whole band."

"Hey!" the kid called after her. "I'm a fan. You have to pose for a photo."

"Yeah, come on, Ronnie," Tina said, her eyes pleading as she tugged on Veronica's sleeve.

It didn't feel right having Tina call her Ronnie. That was a pet name only her closest friends and family used. And it definitely didn't feel right having her use that special name when she was trying to manipulate her to do something she didn't want to do.

"Listen, Tina," Veronica asked, "do you want to get those clothes or not?"

Suddenly Tina forgot all about their fan. "Of course I do."

"Well then, it looks like we need to hit Marlene's Boutique right now."

The two girls scurried over to the boutique. They had assumed that their fan would just give up and leave, but he followed them all the way to the store.

"Do either of you know that young man?" the salesclerk asked as she rang up their purchases.

"Who?" Veronica wondered, turning to look in the direction that the clerk nodded. The fan was standing outside the shop, leaning against the glass and staring at them. "Oh! Um . . . not really," she said.

"Well, he's smearing our window. Why is he leaning against it like that?" the clerk wondered. "He's acting very peculiar. I think I should call mall security."

"No!" Tina practically shouted. "Don't do that!"

"Calm down!" Veronica told her in her sternest voice. "That guy is obviously unhinged. Maybe she should call security."

"We can't do that," Tina insisted. "We don't want the word to get out that we think we're too good for our fans. Let's just go pose for a picture and then I'm sure he'll go away."

Veronica rolled her eyes. "Fine." She handed the clerk her credit card and then turned back to the drummer. "But I want you to know, being in The Candy Hearts is a lot less fun now that it's started ruining my shopping."

XOXO

Betty sat in her family's living room with Tina. She played her guitar while Tina jumped about the room.

"That's not quite right," Betty said, giving her guitar another strum. "Here, let's try it in G. Maybe that'll work." She played the tune again.

"Good. That's a lot better. That's really good," Tina said, bouncing up and down on the couch. She was so excited about the new song they were working on that she couldn't sit still.

Betty glanced over at the clock on the mantelpiece in her family's living room. "Oops! We'd better get going. We're going to be late for practice."

"Oh yeah," Tina said, jumping to her feet. "Practice. Is that tonight?"

"I thought it was." Betty furrowed her brow. "You're the de facto band manager. Don't we have practice tonight?"

"Uh . . . sure we do," Tina replied. "We'd better head over to Veronica's. We can take my car."

Ten minutes later they were standing on the front steps of the Lodge Mansion, ringing the doorbell over and over.

"Where is she?" Betty wondered aloud. "It's not like Veronica to blow us off like this."

"I don't know," Tina shrugged. "She was acting kind of weird when we were at the mall earlier."

Betty turned to look at her. "You guys were at the mall today?"

"Yeah. Why?"

"Oh nothing . . . ," Betty mumbled. "I just wonder where she is now."

Tina sighed. "I guess she's blowing us off."

"No," Betty replied. "She wouldn't do that."

"Are you sure?" Tina gave her a hard look. "I mean, Veronica is kind of a self-absorbed daddy's girl, don't you think?"

"No, not really." Betty shook her head. What was Tina talking about? Veronica was her best friend. She would never admit that Veronica was spoiled or selfish or anything, even if she thought it were true.

"Sure she is. I mean, come on. She wanted to call our band the Veronicas," Tina insisted.

Betty couldn't help but laugh at that. "Yeah, I guess she can *sometimes* be a little self-absorbed, but she's not that bad." She gave it some thought. "Still, it is kind of weird that she's standing us up."

"She probably doesn't think the band is as important as we do."

Giving up on getting anyone to answer the door, Betty walked down the steps and back to the car. "I guess we should just go home."

"Well," Tina said, jumping down the last few steps to join her, "we could go to Pop's Chocklit Shoppe if you wanted. I mean, we might as well have some fun, right?"

"Sure," Betty agreed. She had a craving for the perfect chocolate shake.

XOXO

Pop's Chocklit Shoppe was crowded with teenagers when the girls arrived. "We'll never find a table," Betty said.

"Oh, hey, isn't that Archie?" Tina asked, waving at a redhead in the crowd.

"Yeah, that's him," Betty said, noting that Archie was apparently entertaining Cheryl Blossom.

"Hey, girls," Archie called, signaling them to come over. "Tina, have you met Cheryl Blossom? Cheryl, this is Tina. She's the drummer for The Candy Hearts."

"Hello," Cheryl said, tossing her bouncy, red hair over one shoulder. "Betty, I had heard you managed to get your little band together. It must be fun for you to get a little attention for once."

All Betty could manage to do was blush, but Tina wasn't having it. "Little band?" she said. "The Candy Hearts play three or four times a week. *And* we're playing the Central Town Mall's grand reopening."

"Really? I didn't know you were playing that," Cheryl said, trying to look unimpressed.

"Well you must live in a cave because The Candy Hearts have been playing gigs all over town," Tina told her.

"I'll have you know that our *cave* has six bedrooms, four bathrooms, and a pool," Cheryl smirked. "What's your cave like?"

"Are you girls meeting anyone?" Archie interrupted. "Would you like to join us?"

"Sure, that'd be great." Tina pulled up a chair.

Betty scanned the room for another chair, but the place was so crowded there were none to be found. "Here, you can have my chair, Betty," Cheryl said, getting to her feet. "Archie was just keeping me company while I was waiting for a friend, but I see he just walked in." Cheryl disappeared from the table before anyone could say anything else.

"BFF!" someone shouted as Betty took her seat. Betty hunched her shoulders and blushed furiously. She just wanted to spend some quiet time with her friends, hanging out and having fun like they used to. But Tina turned and smiled, trying to make eye contact with as many people as she could.

"What's the matter, Betty?" Archie asked her.

Betty grimaced, "It's nothing really. I'm just tired of being recognized everywhere I go. I mean, it's like every Candy Hearts fan knows exactly where we're going and what we're doing every second of the day."

Turning back to the table, Tina gave her bandmate a funny look. "I just don't get you, Betty. We're famous. At least in Riverdale, right? I love the attention. Don't you?"

"No." Betty shook her head adamantly, causing her long, blond ponytail to swing from side to side. "I hate it. The whole being recognized thing really creeps me out."

"If you didn't want fans and fame and attention, then why did you form a band?" Tina asked, confused.

"Because I thought it would be fun. And it is fun. Sometimes. I mean, I love playing and writing songs. I just don't like people bothering me all the time. Is it so hard to understand that I just want to be left alone?"

"That's crazy talk," Tina told her as she smiled over her shoulder at a table of boys who were holding up a heart made out of construction paper that had the band's name emblazoned across it.

"Sounds like you just need a break from the music biz, Betty," Archie told her. "Let's get some dinner tomorrow night. I promise there will be absolutely no mention of music. We can even go someplace out of town so that no one recognizes you."

Betty's mood brightened. "Really? That would be great."

"Yeah, that sounds fantastic," Tina added.

"Oh," Archie said slowly. "Of course, you can come, too, if you'd like, Tina. I mean, I can ask Reggie if he wants to be your date. Or maybe Jughead."

"How about trying Reggie first?" Tina suggested with a wink.

"Maybe we should ask Ronnie, too?" Betty suggested.

"No," Tina said quickly, smiling at another table of The Candy Hearts' fans. "Veronica told me this morning that she's going out to dinner with her parents tomorrow night. In fact, she's going to be busy all day."

"Really?" Betty frowned. "She never said anything to me."

"Oh well," Tina said with a shrug. "So where do you guys want to go?"

"I've heard The Landmark in Midvale is good. We could go there," Archie suggested.

Betty broke into a big smile. "Really? I hear it's supergood. I've always wanted to go there."

"Great." Archie leaned back in his chair and folded his hands behind his head. "Then The Landmark it is."

XOXO

The next night, Veronica and Nancy sat waiting in Veronica's pool house.

"Where are they?" Veronica asked, slumping in a lounge chair. "Practice was supposed to start twenty minutes ago."

"I'm sure they'll be here," Nancy assured her, also taking a seat. "Betty doesn't just blow off band practice, and Tina is practically married to the band."

"Try calling Betty again, would you?"

Nancy shook her head. "I just tried her house and her cell. She's not answering."

"How about Tina?"

"I tried her cell and I think she must have it

turned off." Nancy leaned back in her chair and tucked her shapely, cocoa-brown legs under her. "I don't have her home number. Do you?"

"No," Veronica grumbled. "But Tina definitely knows we have practice tonight because we talked about it yesterday at the mall."

"Weird," Nancy agreed. "I hope they're all right."

XOXO

Meanwhile, at The Landmark in Midvale, Archie pulled out a large, red leather chair so Betty could have a seat. "Mademoiselle," he said with a smile.

"Thank you," Betty replied. She giggled as she settled into her seat. Archie was really playing up being the perfect gentleman.

Reggie did not help Tina with her chair. But he made up for it by saying, "You girls look lovely this evening," which caused both Tina and Betty to giggle.

There was an abrupt flash of light and Betty looked up, startled. Blobs of light from the flash of some kid's camera danced in her eyes, but she was able to make out that there was a young girl standing next to her chair, shoving a pen and a heart-shaped piece of paper in her face. "I love The Candy Hearts!" the girl squealed. "Can I have your autograph?"

"Um, sure," Betty said. She fumbled for the paper as another camera flash went off in her face. "What are you doing?!" she demanded.

"I just want your picture. All my friends have total crushes on you guys. They're never going to believe that I actually got to meet you!" the boy crowed.

Reggie stood up. "Get lost!" he shouted at the boy.

Their table was quickly swarmed by kids brandishing cameras and autograph books. "The Candy Hearts are awesome!" one girl trilled.

"I know you guys are going to be totally famous!" another boy shouted as he shoved a camera in Tina's face.

Tina didn't mind the attention at all. She just smiled and signed anything that was shoved at her. Reggie half wished they had already eaten because then he could probably trick her into signing for the check.

"Come on, Betty," Archie said, jumping to his feet. "Let's get out of here!" They made a dash to Archie's old car with the fans in hot pursuit.

Once they were safely inside the vehicle with all the doors locked, Tina began to laugh. "Did you see how many fans we have? That was awesome!"

But Betty was not happy. She had been looking forward to a nice dinner with no talk of bands or songs or fans, and now the evening was ruined.

"How do they keep finding us?" Betty wondered, her voice trembling. "And why do they keep finding us? Is it really worth mobbing us and ruining our dinner for a few autographs? I mean, no one even knows us outside of Riverdale."

Tina rolled her eyes. "Betty, you are totally underestimating the power of The Candy Hearts."

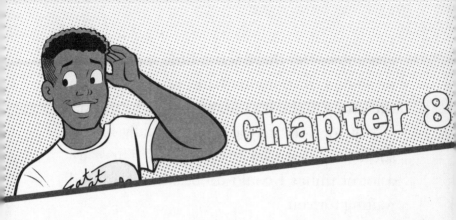

Chapter 8

"Where were you?" Veronica all but shouted the next day as she unlocked her car's trunk so Betty could put in her guitar. "Nancy and I waited for you guys yesterday for *two hours!*"

"Ronnie, what are you talking about?" Betty stared at her, wide-eyed. "Band practice wasn't yesterday. It was the day before. Tina and I came over, but you weren't home."

"That's a lie! I specifically told Tina I was going to the club with my parents and we agreed that practice would be yesterday. Nancy knew about it. Why didn't you?"

Betty was already stressed. She wasn't in the mood to be the target of one of Veronica's temper tantrums. "Oh just calm down," Betty grumbled. "So there was a little mistake and we ended up thinking band practice was on the wrong night. It's not the end of the world."

"Not for you, maybe, but I actually have a social life," Veronica informed her. "There are a lot of things I could do besides sit around waiting for you."

"Like what, Miss Popularity?"

"I could have gone on a date with Archie." Veronica unlocked the car and they both climbed in.

Betty laughed. "No, you couldn't have."

"And why not?" Veronica snarled as she started up her car.

"Because," Betty told her, buckling her seatbelt, "Archie was on a date with me."

Veronica was stunned into silence. She was so furious and confused and hurt that she couldn't think of anything to say to her best friend. She couldn't even look at her. They drove to Pop's Chocklit Shoppe in an uncomfortable silence that continued even after they met Tina and Nancy.

"You guys, please talk to each other," Tina

pleaded as The Candy Hearts set up their gear at the back of Pop's Chocklit Shoppe. "This is all my fault. I got confused when Veronica said she was going out to dinner with her family. I switched the days in my head. Don't be mad at each other."

"Or"—Veronica directed her comment at Tina although it was obvious she wanted Betty to overhear—"somebody wanted me to sit at home waiting so she could sneak off and have a date with Archie."

"Hey," Betty said, whirling around to face both of them. "Archie asked me out and I said yes. We were going to invite you, but Tina said you were busy."

Tina looked sheepish. "Sorry. I really thought last night was when you were going out with your folks."

Veronica glared at the girls. "I'm not sure I believe either one of you."

XOXO

That night, the show at Pop's Chocklit Shoppe was pretty awful. Betty and Veronica's harmonies were painfully off. Even their voices weren't getting along. Tina raced through every song and Nancy just seemed lost. When it was time for them to play their most popular song, "BFF," Betty glanced over, half-willing to put their argument behind her and share the microphone with Veronica like she always did, but Ronnie glared at her so angrily, she just stayed where she was.

After their performance, Tina was bouncing off the walls as was her custom after a show. "That was great!" she said.

Nancy gave her a concerned look. "Great? What are you talking about? I'm completely embarrassed. We sounded awful."

"Okay, we didn't sound our best," the drummer conceded. "But tons of kids asked for our autographs and someone sent us each a red rose and I saw at least three girls and two guys wearing homemade Candy Heart T-shirts. We should really get some professional band T-shirts made up and sell them at the shows."

There was a sincere lack of enthusiasm for her latest idea. Veronica just rolled her eyes and Betty busied herself with packing up her guitar. Nancy took a deep breath and then said, "Tina, maybe we should, you know, ease up a little with the whole band thing. I mean, playing so many gigs all the time is kind of stressful. The parents for all of my babysitting jobs are mad at me, and I haven't seen Chuck in a week."

Tina looked like she could have been knocked over with a feather. "Ease up on the band? Are you crazy? If anything we've got to start practicing a lot more. We've got to learn more songs. We've got to give this band everything we've got, right?!"

Raising both her shoulders in a questioning shrug, Nancy asked, "But why?"

"Why?" Tina was flabbergasted. "Why? Because we've got the huge mall gig in less than a week and The Candy Hearts have got to be perfect. That show is going to open a lot of doors for us, right? We're going to be playing all the time. And bigger shows. Much bigger. After things go well at the mall, we are going to get a ton of great gigs."

"Hmmm." Nancy pursed her lips. "Tina,

I've got to be honest with you, summer is almost over and in another couple of weeks we'll be back at school. Then I'm really going to need to focus on homework and college applications. I can't spend all my free time on the band."

Tina crossed her arms. "So what are you saying, Nancy? Are you trying to quit the band? Because if that's what you're saying, we can always find another bass player."

Pinching the bridge of her nose, Nancy shook her head. "Listen, I don't know what I'm saying. I'm tired and I just want to go home and, you know, not think about the band for a little while."

"Good idea," Betty agreed, hoisting up her guitar case.

"I could go a few days without thinking about the band," Veronica chimed in.

They all headed for the door. "Hey, guys," Tina called after them. "Don't forget we have practice tomorrow."

"Oh, I won't forget," Veronica said over her shoulder. "I'm just wondering if *you* will."

Veronica drove Betty home in almost total silence. It was an even more uncomfortable car ride than it had been on the way to Pop's Chocklit Shoppe.

Betty slouched in her seat, counting the seconds until it was over. She wasn't feeling very good about The Candy Hearts anymore. Mostly it was the obsessive fans. She just couldn't figure out how the teenagers kept tracking them down. And, more importantly, why? But, up until that evening, at least playing the shows had been fun. But now with Veronica not even willing to share a microphone with her during "BFF," the best thing about the band had suddenly soured. Betty didn't know what to do. Normally when she had a problem she talked to Veronica. But the icy chill radiating off of her best friend let Betty know that remedy was not currently an option.

XOXO

Practice the next day brought little relief to the band tension. Fans hiding in the shrubbery kept a steady racket going of "plink, plink, plink" as they pelted the windows of the pool house with personalized candy hearts. The sweets said things like "BFF," "I luv you," and "You're mine." It was creepy on a couple of levels. Veronica had to use the pool house phone to call the butler and get him to chase the kids off with his broom again.

"Why does this keep happening?" Betty asked. "I mean, we're just a local band. We should be begging our friends to come to our shows, not being stalked by candy-wielding weirdos."

"You're right," Veronica agreed. "This whole obsessive fan thing has officially gotten old."

"You guys," Tina said, putting her hands on her hips, "they're *fans*. Don't you get it? You're supposed to be flattered. They love our music, right? They're obsessed with us. Doesn't that make you feel good?"

The other members of The Candy Hearts gave her concerned looks. "Not really," Nancy admitted.

A stunned look crossed Tina's face. "I can't believe what I'm hearing! Do you know how many girls would kill to be in your position?"

"Would you please relax?" Veronica said impatiently. "We're all going to be starting school in a couple of weeks. You included. I'm starting to think that's a good thing. Then maybe you'll have something to obsess over besides the band."

XOXO

Betty looked at her reflection in the mirror and sighed. The outfits Veronica had picked out for The Candy Hearts to wear for the Central Town Mall grand reopening were supercute, but there was no sparkle in Betty's blue eyes. This was the big gig they'd all been working for, but she couldn't help but feel nervous. Central High was Riverdale's school rival, and there was always a chance that the audience would give them a chilly reception. And, even worse, there was a bigger chance that Veronica would give her the cold shoulder onstage.

Smoothing down her minidress, Betty gave her outfit one last check. Something kept itching the back of her neck at the collar line. Running her hand across the cloth, Betty found a tag that she quickly clipped off. She went to throw it away, but then did a double take. Veronica had told her that she'd purchased the band's outfits at Forever Seventeen, but the tag definitely said Marlene's Boutique. Betty frowned as a large pang of guilt washed over her. Veronica had felt the need to lie to her about where she purchased their outfits. They'd been friends since before either one of them knew the difference between a designer label and something from a bargain basement, and now, all of a sudden, Veronica felt the need to lie. Betty couldn't help but feel that being in The Candy Hearts was driving a wedge into their friendship. The whole thing just made her feel sad.

The parking lot of Central Town Mall was already filled with cars by the time Tina picked Betty up and they drove over together.

"Wow, people are really excited," Betty mused, looking out the window.

"Of course they are!" Tina wheeled the car into the back lot where Ms. Marcos had instructed them to park. "They've even hired roadies to help us with our gear."

"Roadies?" Betty perked up. "Cool! The closest we've come to roadies is when The Archies help carry our speakers."

"I know!" Tina was grinning from ear to ear. "The Candy Hearts are really coming up in the world. This gig is just the beginning."

The comment caused Betty to purse her lips, but she said nothing. The mall show meant a lot to Tina and she wanted her friend to have her moment—even if Betty wasn't all that enthusiastic about sharing in the moment.

Veronica and Nancy were already backstage setting up their gear when Tina and Betty walked in, followed by three enormous roadies toting their equipment. "You can put my kit down over there." Tina beamed at the roadie who had somehow managed to carry the four heavy cases that contained her entire drum set. "I could get used to this," Tina said, winking at Nancy, who was standing nearby feeling awkward as a huge roadie loomed over her.

Nancy peered up at the hulking man. "It might take me awhile."

"Don't be so small town," Tina said, laughing at her.

"You live in Riverdale, too, you know," Nancy pointed out. "And speaking of which, have any of you gotten a look at the crowd? There are a *ton* of kids from Central out there. I mean, the place is packed and practically the whole first six rows next to the stage are kids from Central High."

"So." Tina shrugged as she opened one of her drum cases.

"Tina, you don't exactly know this because you just moved here, but Central and Riverdale are huge rivals," Nancy informed her.

This made Tina laugh again. "You're being ridiculous. The Candy Hearts' music transcends silly high school rivalries. We have nothing to worry about."

"If you say so," Nancy replied, but she didn't sound convinced.

"Hey, Veronica," Betty said as she walked toward her maybe/maybe-not best friend. Her initial attempt was met with a cold shoulder, but Betty forged ahead, anyway. "Thanks for the Marlene's Boutique outfit. Everyone looks really cute."

The comment brought Veronica up short. "They're from Forever Seventeen."

"No," Betty said, keeping her voice gentle, "they're not. There was a tag on my minidress that you must have missed. It said Marlene's."

Veronica stumbled for an explanation.

"Oh, Ronnie," Tina interjected. "Why don't you just tell her the truth?"

Veronica knitted her brows. "What are you talking about?"

"Oh please," Tina said, rolling her eyes. Then, she turned to Betty. "Veronica was worried you'd get bent out of shape if you knew how much our outfits cost because, you know, you're kind of a goody-two-shoes."

"I never said that!" Veronica insisted.

"Come on, Ronnie," Tina said defiantly. "I'm sick of you two fighting. Let's be honest here and clear the air."

Glaring right back at her, Veronica snarled, "Stop calling me Ronnie."

Betty's cheeks grew pink. She looked

over at Veronica and said, "You called me a goody-two-shoes?"

"No . . ." Veronica wanted to explain, but Tina cut her off.

"Not in so many words, but come on, Betty. You are kind of a goody-two-shoes. Accept it. Just like what you said about Veronica. She's kind of a spoiled daddy's girl."

Veronica whipped her head around to glare at her friend. "You called me a spoiled daddy's girl?"

"No!" Betty insisted. "I didn't."

Tina chuckled. "Yes, you did. I mean, maybe not word-for-word, but you might as well admit how you feel. *Spoiled daddy's girl* is what you're thinking when you look at Veronica. We all are."

"I am not thinking that!" Betty protested, her face glowing fire engine–red. "I would never think something like that about Veronica. She's my best friend."

"Not anymore!" Veronica thundered.

"Would you two please stop fighting all the time?" Tina yelled at them both. "I am so tired of you guys always being at each other's throats! I hate being in the middle!" Tina yanked her Tri-Tom out of its case. "Why do I always have to do everything around here? Why am I always in the middle?"

Betty and Veronica both turned to give her questioning looks. Then, with a sideways glance, Veronica asked under her breath, "Do you have any idea what she's talking about?"

Shaking her head, Betty replied, "Not really."

XOXO

By the time The Candy Hearts were all set up, the crowd was getting impatient. Someone started chanting, "BFF! BFF!" and soon the whole crowd chimed in.

Looking at her watch, Nancy frowned and clucked her tongue. "It's only twelve thirty. We're not supposed to start playing until one. What's everyone doing here already? How are we supposed to do our sound check?"

"What can I say?" Tina threw her hands up in the air as if she were at a loss, but it was obvious she was thrilled. "We've got great fans."

"Girls, what are you doing?" Ms. Marcos called as she rushed over to them.

"Trying to figure out how to do our sound check," Nancy offered.

"Well, I'm afraid it's too crowded for that. You'll just have to do without," Ms. Marcos replied.

"But we have to have a sound check," Veronica insisted. "We have to know if our mics are working and how everything sounds with the mixing board. Betty and Nancy have to make sure they're in tune. I'm sorry, Ms. Marcos, but we really do need one."

The mall manager appeared even more strained as she looked at the girls' faces and then glanced at the curtain that was doing little to muffle the sound of the crowd chanting, "BFF! BFF!"

"No we don't," Tina interjected. "Not really. Don't worry, Ms. Marcos, The Candy Hearts are professionals and we're going to sound great even if we don't have a sound check."

"What?" Veronica glared at the drummer. "Are you crazy?"

"Not as crazy as that crowd is about The Candy Hearts. Come on, girls. We just need to have confidence and play, right? Listen to them out there. The crowd already loves us."

"Okay, fine." Veronica gave in. "Let's just get this over with. Nancy, what time is it?"

Nancy looked at her watch. "We've got twenty minutes before we hit the stage."

"Excuse me a minute, girls." Ms. Marcos hurried over to the stage manager.

Betty peeked through the break in the curtain and scanned the audience. Turning pale, she put a hand to her forehead and murmured, "I think I'm going to be sick."

She really did look ill and Tina was immediately alarmed. "What? Why?"

"Because there are two billion kids out there, a ton of them are from Central, and we haven't even had a sound check," Betty wailed. "I hate to say it, but The Candy Hearts are going down in flames."

"Don't be ridiculous!" Tina shouted. "There's a lot riding on this show! We have to make it our best show ever!"

"BFF! BFF!" the crowd kept chanting.

Looking grim, Veronica grumbled under her breath, "I wish we'd never agreed to this."

Ms. Marcos hurried back over to The Candy Hearts. "Girls, we're going to start the show early," she informed them.

"What?!" The Candy Hearts collectively gasped.

"Those kids out there are going to start eating the stage if we don't do something. This whole thing is turning into a safety hazard. You girls have got to get out there and start playing."

"But . . ." Betty floundered.

"Now!" Ms. Marcos insisted, herding them onto the stage.

Stumbling forward, the girls hurried to man their instruments. Betty barely had time to strap on her guitar before the curtains parted and the lights came up. There was a man's voice announcing over the PA system. "Ladies and gentlemen, The Candy Hearts!"

Chapter 9

A giant roar from the audience crashed over The Candy Hearts as they tried to get their bearings. Betty stared at the standing room only crowd. All the girls froze.

"Play something!" Ms. Marcos yelled from the wings.

Tina held her sticks over her head, clicked them together, and counted off. "One, two, three, four!"

The first song on The Candy Heart's playlist was "Surfer Boys." At least it was supposed to be. Betty could barely hear the other members of the band over the racket the audience was making. Suddenly her guitar made a weird "pling!" noise and Betty jumped back, slightly startled. She looked down at her instrument. "That was weird," she said to herself. Then she felt a small pain on her head. Something was definitely wrong. Betty looked over to see Nancy flinch as she was hit in the cheek with something.

Oh no, Betty thought. *Some kids from Central High must be trying to ruin our show by throwing stuff at the stage.*

Another projectile came zooming at her and Betty ducked out of the way. She got a look at the strange pellet as it went skittering across the stage floor.

Suddenly she understood. They were not being harassed by kids from Central High intent on ruining the show. She'd just been targeted with a pastel candy heart.

The candies rained down, hitting faster and harder until The Candy Hearts were trying to perform in a hailstorm of treats. As "Surfer Boys" came to a ragged close, Nancy held up her hand to shield her face. "This is awful! Why are they doing this?"

"Try to think of it as a compliment," Tina

called from behind the drums. The candy hitting her cymbals was keeping a steady rhythm.

"It's hard to think of people whipping candy at your head as a compliment!" Nancy shouted back.

"What do we do?" Betty asked as she put up a hand to try to ward off the sweets.

"Keep playing!" Tina insisted.

"Really?" Betty was surprised. It didn't make sense to just stand there and let rabid fans use them for target practice.

She couldn't even imagine why fans would think pelting them with edible hearts was a good idea. Maybe it was actually a sneak attack from their rival high school? If that was true, it was a pretty clever way to go about doing it.

But no, the crowd was cheering. They wanted to see The Candy Hearts play. They somehow thought whipping candy at the band was a good idea.

"BFF! BFF!" the crowd chanted again.

"Hey, girls," Veronica shouted as she pulled a candy out of her hair, "are we taking requests?"

"I say if they want the song then we give it to them!" Tina shouted back.

"Fine by me!" Nancy added. "At this rate, I don't think we're going to make it through our playlist!"

A candy heart bounced off Betty's temple, dangerously close to her left eye. She felt her nose begin to burn and her eyes starting to water.

She didn't want to be a baby about the whole thing, but she just couldn't help it. Forming The Candy Hearts was supposed to be about having some fun with her best friend. Now Veronica hated her, plus she was trapped onstage while rabid fans used her for candy target practice.

"Betty!" Tina called, breaking her out of her tearful reverie. "Pull it together! We're going to play 'BFF'! One, two, three, four!"

Betty stepped up to the microphone and sang:

Finally hit the weekend
Hanging with my best friend
Listenin' to the radio

Recognizing the opening strains of their favorite song, the crowd went wild. The number of candy treats that were being thrown at the stage tripled.

Veronica tried to shield herself from the deluge by half turning her back to the audience. "This is ridiculous," she growled to herself, barely able to continue playing her keyboard.

Either the candy shower had to stop or the show had to stop, but she wasn't going to tolerate being pelted to death by pastel-colored treats. Suddenly the C and D notes on Veronica's keyboard jammed. She'd depressed the keys, but they wouldn't rise again. Between the painful downpour and the malfunctioning instrument, Veronica lost her place in the song. She struggled to find it, but then gave up and stopped playing completely.

The rest of the band petered out quickly after that. There were a few seconds of absolute quiet and then the audience started to boo.

"What's going on?" Betty's voice cut through the noise.

Veronica looked up sharply, ready to tear Betty's head off. But then she noticed that there were tear tracks on her best friend's face.

"My keyboard's stuck," she said in a much kinder voice than she had initially intended to use. Feeling around the notes to figure out the problem, Veronica discovered a pastel heart that had wedged itself beneath the black half-note between the C and D. Prying out the sweet, Veronica was about to cast it aside when she noticed something.

The letters written on the heart were *BFF*.

She was standing on a stage, struggling through a song that her former best friend wrote about their friendship while a crazed audience chucked candy at them.

The heart that stopped the show suddenly reminded Veronica of all of Betty's good qualities. She really and truly was her best friend forever. And here Veronica had been letting petty arguments about the band ruin their friendship. The entire situation was just too ludicrous.

The whole thing suddenly struck Veronica as being very funny.

Veronica started smiling and then she started laughing. All the anger and hurt feelings she felt toward Betty just melted away. She instantly understood that whatever petty grievances had come between them were more than likely just simple misunderstandings. Veronica suddenly felt very silly for not realizing this fact in the first place.

The crowd grew impatient and started up their chant again. "BFF! BFF!"

Veronica knew they needed to go on with the show, but she was laughing so hard she found it impossible to straighten up and play.

Tina yelled at her, "What are you doing? Get it together! You're ruining the show!" The statement was so ludicrous it made the keyboarder laugh even harder.

"BFF! BFF!"

"Betty!" Veronica called across the stage. "Hey, Betty!" Betty looked up and Veronica waved her over. "Come over here for a minute. Will you?"

"BFF! BFF!"

Her face stained with tears, Betty hurried across the stage. "What is it?" she wondered. "What's wrong?"

"Well we're in serious danger of being pelted to death by candy hearts. That's not so great," Veronica told her.

"What?" Betty's blue eyes glistened with tears under the spotlights.

Veronica realized that the guitarist was in a very fragile state and it wasn't the time to make sarcastic remarks. So, instead, she held out the key-jamming candy heart toward Betty. "Here, look what got stuck in my keyboard."

Betty squinted at the treat. "Yeah, a heart candy. I don't know if you've noticed, but they're everywhere," she explained as more candy went whizzing by her head.

Even so, Veronica gestured at the heart. "Well read this one."

Looking down, Betty mouthed the letters *BFF*.

"As in you're my BFF," Veronica explained.

Betty looked up, her eyes wide. "I am?"

Rolling her eyes, Veronica laughed. "Of course you are!" Then, becoming more serious, she added, "I'm sorry I got so angry with you. I think I was mostly jealous because you were spending so much time with Tina."

"Well I'm sorry if I made you feel jealous. Tina's just so demanding about writing songs and working on the band. Plus you know I have trouble saying no to people." Betty smiled sheepishly.

Veronica acknowledged this statement with a nod. "I know you do. I should have been more understanding."

"Me too," Betty added. "And I shouldn't have let Tina take over like she did."

"Can we please just forget all that and start being friends again?" Veronica asked.

"Of course!" Betty threw her arms around Veronica's neck and they hugged. "You're my best friend!"

The crowd was reaching an earsplitting noise level. "BFF! BFF!"

"Betty! Veronica!" Tina shouted from behind her drum kit. "What are you guys doing?! There's time to chat after the show! We're on stage right now playing a gig." She pointed toward the audience. "Remember?"

"BFF! BFF!"

Betty and Veronica both turned and looked out at the crowd. "Come on," Veronica said, her arm still slung around Betty's shoulder. "Let's do this." Betty was about to head back across the stage to her own microphone, but Veronica stopped her. "Hey! Where are you going? Stay here and sing with me."

Veronica leaned forward and said into the mic, "Ladies and gentlemen, I'm afraid we're going to have to call a do-over." Light laughter rippled over the audience. "If you would please hold your cheers and the throwing of candy hearts until after the show, we would appreciate it." This made the audience chuckle a little harder.

Tina held her drumsticks over her head, clicked them together, and counted off. "One, two, three, four!"

The song started. Betty and Veronica leaned into their shared microphone and sang:

Finally hit the weekend
Hanging with my best friend
Listenin' to the radio
Talking fast and cruisin' slow
Doesn't matter where we go!

When they got to the refrain, Betty glanced over at Veronica. Her best friend was smiling back at her and Betty knew everything was going to be all right. And when they sang the chorus, she knew they both really meant it.

'Cause you're my best frie . . . hend!
You're my best frie . . . hend!
You're my best friend!

XOXO

The Candy Hearts took their bows in a hailstorm of sweets and then ran for the wings of the stage.

"You know," Veronica said, shaking a few candies out of her hair, "if they're going to throw something, why don't they throw jewelry?"

Betty laughed. "Or maybe we should have gone with Kitten Heel because then they'd throw shoes."

"I don't know about that," Nancy said, unstrapping her bass. "Shoes hurt."

"So listen," Betty said when she had packed up her gear and had a moment to speak to Veronica alone, "I hope you're not going to be mad, but I think this was my farewell performance with The Candy Hearts. I love playing music, but I find all the gigs and the obsessive fans *way* too stressful." Betty gave her friend an apprehensive look. "Are you mad?"

"No." Veronica broke into a smile. "I'm not mad at all. To be honest, I was thinking the exact same thing. Being in The Candy Hearts just isn't that fun anymore. I mean, I'm going to be really bummed about not being in a band and I'm going to miss a lot of the attention, but I've got to keep my grades up for college. Plus, besides playing, I don't feel like we do anything for fun anymore. The Candy Hearts just feels like too much work."

"That's a relief," Betty said, returning her smile. "I was nervous about telling you. I should have known you felt the same way."

"I guess we'd better tell Tina and Nancy."

Betty sighed, not looking forward to Tina's reaction. "Yep. Let's get this over with."

"Where is Tina, anyway?" Veronica asked, looking around. "Nancy, have you seen Tina?"

Nancy looked up from wrapping cords. "No. She said something about a meeting, then disappeared. That was about ten minutes ago."

"Well I guess we can just tell you first then." Veronica walked over so she could look Nancy in the eye. "Betty and I have decided that we want to leave the band."

"What?" Nancy's big brown eyes went wide with surprise.

"Yeah, sorry." Betty joined in. "I just can't handle the fans anymore and with school about to start . . ."

"No, no, no," Nancy interrupted her. "I didn't mean *what* as in bad, I meant *what* as in good."

Her comment perplexed the other girls. "What?"

Nancy let her shoulders sag with the relief of finally confessing. "I've been wanting to quit the band for like a month, but I didn't know how to break it to you guys."

"Okay good," Veronica said. "Then we're all in agreement: We're going to break up the band."

"What?!" Tina shouted, storming over to them. "Did I just hear what I think I heard? You want to break up the band?!"

Chapter 10

All three girls were startled by Tina's outburst, but Veronica was the first to find her voice. "Um, yeah. We were just talking about it. I'm sorry, but being in The Candy Hearts just isn't that much fun anymore."

Betty stepped in to support her friend. "Plus, school's starting again, and, you know, that'll mean studying and school activities and stuff."

"But the band can't break up now! It just can't!" Tina insisted. She looked like she was on the verge of tears. "I was just coming over to tell you guys some fantastic news and now you're all here trying to mutiny!"

"Oh, um." Betty felt her guilty reflexes kicking in. "What's the good news?"

"Well," Tina said after taking a deep breath, "I didn't tell you guys before because I didn't want to make you nervous, right? But there was a talent manager in the crowd tonight. He loved the show! He's offered to rep us and he can book us six gigs in New York City starting next week! Isn't that fantastic?"

"Tina," Veronica said, annoyed, "you knew the rest of us wanted to start playing fewer gigs. Not more."

"And not gigs in New York," Betty said.

"Yeah," Nancy added. "My parents will never go for that."

"Oh yes they will!" Tina insisted. "If they know how important it is to you."

Nancy put a steadying arm on Tina's shoulder. "I'm sorry, but it's just *not* that important to me."

Tina was furious. "What are you talking about?! If being famous isn't that important to you, then what is?"

"Getting good grades so I can get into a good college," Nancy said without hesitation. She went on, "Spending time with Chuck before the summer is completely over. I'm sorry, but I didn't join The Candy Hearts to become famous. I just wanted to have some fun."

"Yeah, Tina," Betty said. "I'm sorry, but I think we all feel the same way."

Stamping her foot, Tina pouted. "Come on! Just do the six shows in New York with me and we'll see how things go after that."

Betty shook her head. "I don't think so. I'm sorry, but it's probably better if we just end things now."

Tina's face flushed with anger. "Better for you guys, maybe, but not better for me! I can't believe you're stabbing me in the back after all the hard work I've been doing!" She glared at the three of them. "You have to go to New York! You guys owe me!"

Caught off guard, Veronica felt compelled to defend herself and the other girls. "Tina, what are you talking about? We've all put a lot of work into the band. I mean, you did book most of our gigs, but we all worked hard."

"Ha!" Tina scoffed. "You guys have had it easy compared to me."

Folding her arms, Veronica leveled the drummer with a flat gaze. "Oh, really? And just what extra work were you doing that we're all so blissfully unaware of?"

Tina looked like her head might explode. "Are you kidding me?! I mean, really, are you kidding?!" She began listing tasks off on her fingers. "I book all the gigs. If it was up to you guys, we would have only had a few gigs a month. I had to practically bully you guys into practicing half the time. I nearly wrote half the songs. I named the band. I designed the band's appearance."

"Wait a minute," Veronica interrupted. "I'm the one that bought all our outfits. I think I deserve credit for the band's appearance."

"You just supplied the plastic!" Tina shouted. "I'm the one that did scouting trips to the mall and then had to figure out different ways to get you there so you'd buy them. *And* I had to keep Betty from freaking out because of all the money you were spending."

Veronica was stunned. "Wow. I didn't realize you were such a gold digger."

"Well I had to!" Tina insisted. "We couldn't go onstage looking like a bunch of amateurs!"

Betty's eyes narrowed with suspicion, but she tried to keep her voice casual. "So what else did you do for The Candy Hearts?"

"Everything!" Tina replied. "I kept you writing songs. And then I kept you from freaking out just because a few fans started showing you a little attention."

"Is that it?" Nancy asked.

"No, that's not it!" Tina screeched. "Who do you think built up the fan support for The Candy Hearts? Who do you think was on Facebook and Twitter and Craigslist every day letting the fans know about the shows and where we'd be and what we'd be doing? That was me! I was practically tied to the computer all summer letting fans know everything about us. All you guys did was complain about it!"

"And what about these?" Veronica picked a candy heart out of the folds of her minidress and tossed it on the ground between them. "Did you have anything to do with these?"

"You know I did! I practically emptied my bank account ordering them," Tina bellowed. "Do you know how expensive it is to get custom hearts overnighted to Riverdale?"

"Uh, yes," Veronica told her. "As a matter of fact, I do."

Betty's hands were clenched at her sides and she was trembling slightly. "I can't believe you did that! Did you tell people to throw them at us?"

"No!" Tina suddenly registered that she may have revealed too much. "Well not exactly."

"And you told them where we'd be? At dinner or by the pool or wherever. You arranged it so people could harass us?"

It became obvious to Tina that the other members of The Candy Hearts might not be happy with her revelation, but there was no point in denying her tactics any longer. "Well . . . yes," Tina sheepishly confessed.

With her hands on her hips, Veronica glared at the drummer. "So I guess you *have* worked a lot harder on the band than the rest of us."

"I know." Tina nodded her head vigorously.

"*Now* do you see why you have to go to New York?"

Veronica's brown eyes were practically shooting daggers. "No," she snarled, "I do not. And I'm definitely not going."

"Yeah," Betty added. "I'm sorry, Tina, but I don't want to go, either."

"Me neither," Nancy chimed in. "I think fame just isn't as important to us as it is to you."

There were several moments of sputtering before Tina could even speak. When she finally found her words, she screeched, "Fine! I'll form a new band. There are millions of girls out there that would kill for this opportunity!"

Betty softened, realizing that Tina was truly disappointed. "I'm sorry," she said in a gentler voice. "We didn't realize how much you wanted to be famous. I guess it's something we should have talked about when we formed the band."

But Tina was beyond being rational about the disbanding of The Candy Hearts. "The name's mine, you know!" she raged at them while fighting back angry tears. "I came up with it and I'm going to keep it!"

"Fine," Veronica shrugged.

"And most of the songs! I wrote half of them, so I should get them. It's the least you can do after stabbing me in the back!"

"You can have everything you worked on," Betty told her. "But none of the songs that are just mine. Especially 'BFF.'"

"But," Tina protested, "that's our best song!"

Betty held firm. "Sorry, Tina, but there's no way. I wrote that song about Veronica and me before we even really knew you. That's our song."

Epilogue

With the dissolution of the original Candy Hearts, Betty was more than happy to return to her comfortable, although admittedly quieter, life in Riverdale. She had time to reconnect with her family and spend time with friends that she felt like she hadn't seen in ages. Tina had left for New York almost immediately after the mall show without even bothering to say good-bye. Betty felt a bit bad about it, but she understood that Tina was a girl focused on pursuing her dream.

Nancy was out and about with Chuck almost every day. He had apparently decided to take a break from working on his portfolio in order to enjoy the last days of summer.

Betty hadn't seen much of Veronica since the band's breakup. She knew her best friend had gone on a week's vacation with her parents, but she was still concerned that Veronica might be feeling a bit bad about the disbanding of The Candy Hearts. Veronica was the kind of girl that thrived on a lot of attention, after all. That's why Betty felt so pleased when Veronica called her up to see if she wanted to head to Pop's Chocklit Shoppe to see The Archies play. It would be a good opportunity to check in with her best friend to make sure everything was going okay.

"Hello, ladies," Mr. Burly-Man the bouncer said as he stood, blocking the back entrance to Tate's place.

"Yeah, yeah, we know," Veronica rolled her eyes. "Customers go around front."

The bouncer looked a little confused. "No, I was just saying hello. You can go on in." He stepped to one side, unblocking the door.

Both girls stopped and stared at him. "You mean you're not going to give us a hard time about being in the band?" Betty asked.

"No, I recognize you two from The Candy Hearts." He gave them an appreciative smile. "I know you're musicians."

"Well," Veronica murmured to her friend as they sauntered into Pop's Chocklit Shoppe, "that might be our very last perk from being in the band."

"Does that bother you?" Betty asked. "I mean, that we're not in a band anymore? Are you going to miss being in the spotlight?"

"No, I'm happy to be done with The Candy Hearts. Being in a band is always fun, and at first it was kind of neat to have fans and everything, but I really don't want to be famous. There's just no privacy," Veronica confided. "Besides, it was putting *way* too much strain on our friendship."

"Yeah," Betty agreed. "I think Tina had a lot to do with that. I wouldn't say she was a bad person, she was just very . . ." Betty searched for the right word.

"Manipulative?" Veronica offered.

Betty smiled. "Exactly!"

"Hey, girls," Jughead called, loping up to

them. "Boy, do I have something to show you." He pulled out a magazine that he had stuffed in his back pocket and unrolled it. "Look at this."

Betty and Veronica put their heads together over the photo that Jughead was indicating. It was on a page with the headline, "Chicks That Rock!: Up-and-Coming Girl Bands," and among a collage of six photographs was an image of Tina with three other girls, all dressed in jewel tones and wearing bright lipstick. The caption read, "Tina and The Candy Hearts are winning raves with their song 'Best Friends Forever.'"

"Wow!" Betty blinked repeatedly. "She didn't waste any time."

Veronica gave her a concerned look. "Does it bother you that she's pretty much ripping off your song?"

"No." Betty shook her head. "I'm glad she's pursuing her dream." Then she added with a smile, "And not torturing the rest of us in the process."

The Archies' show was pretty packed, but

Betty and Veronica managed to score a table up front, along with Midge; her boyfriend, Moose; and Kevin. When it was time for the band to play "Sugar Sugar," Archie leaned into the microphone and said to the audience, "Our old bandmates, Betty and Veronica, are here. I think maybe if we harass them a little, they'll join us onstage. What do you guys think?"

The crowd started applauding. Veronica looked like she could be persuaded, but Betty hesitated. She looked up, her blue eyes very wide. "Do you really think we should?"

"Oh, come on," Veronica said, pulling her by the arm. "It'll be fun."

And it was. They played "Sugar Sugar." The crowd cheered so much that they went on to play "Jingle Jangle." The crowd kept cheering so they kept playing. Betty and Veronica stayed onstage for the rest of the gig, dancing and laughing and singing.

"That was really fun, you guys," Archie said after the show while the band packed up their gear. "I wish you two would rejoin the band.

I know we're not as glamorous as The Candy Hearts, and we're still going to be called The Archies, but the band's a lot more fun when you're part of it."

Surprised, Betty and Veronica exchanged tentative looks, but the decision was pretty obvious to both of them. "We'd love to join the band again, Archiekins!" Veronica cooed.

"Yeah, that'd be great!" Betty chimed in. "But," she couldn't help but add, "I do have a question."

"What's that?" Archie asked, snapping shut his guitar case.

"Well," Betty hesitated. "I was wondering, why let us back in the band? I mean, we'd love to play with The Archies again, but after everything that's happened, why take us back?"

Archie smiled at them, his eyes twinkling. "Don't you girls get it? What's the point of cake without a little frosting?"

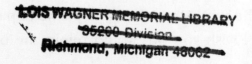